the Light Prince

CHE GILSON

www.sincyrpublishing.com
Shifting culture, one story at a time.

COPYRIGHT

For my two best critique partners - Suzanne and Miriah.

TABLE OF CONTENTS

CHAPTER 1

Peasants came running when they saw Princess Aminira's caravan. It was the same in every country. Men, women, and children left their labors and ran to the edge of the road to gaze, openmouthed, at the passing entourage. Though they didn't know who Princess Aminira was or why such a magnificent retinue passed by, they bowed and curtsied and stared, sure that something grand passed through their lives.

Princess Aminira on her dapper grey mare scanned the crowd carefully and chose to wave to a little girl in a yellow woolen dress and dingy apron. The girl's face lit up and she waved back. Her friends giggled, clearly thrilled by the attention.

"Send them a token," Aminira told Vizier Hamandir, who rode beside her on a placid roan gelding. He had been one of her father's advisors before being sent with Aminira. "Nothing too fine... ivory I think, with ebony embellishment or none at all."

Vizier Hamandir frowned, nose in the air, as though offended by the foreign peasants. They were little different than the peasants of their home land, the Sultanate of Qadarh. At last he nodded and called to one of the servants who walked with the caravan.

Up ahead, a little boy ran alongside one of the guards, his eyes so wide and fixed he tripped over a mile marker half buried in the grass. Unfazed, the boy picked himself up and kept after the guard.

"Why are you so brown?" the boy called.

"Because God made me this color," the guard said stiffly.

"Which god?" the boy asked. Then he held up a pink hand stained with dirt. "The gods made me this color."

"God makes many colors," the guard answered and marched a little faster.

Princess Aminira let the barest smile turn the corner of her lips up. Vizier Hamandir sighed. The Royal guard was trained to be silent when on duty but in these foreign lands, besieged by questions, Princess Aminira had ordered them to answer the people, peasant or noble. Of course there was a difference between answering questions and full on theological debate. Aminira hadn't anticipated the varied beliefs of the northern continent and its pantheon of gods. In Qadarh, there was but one.

"I hope the boy does not ask us all about the color of our skin. We will be in the next kingdom before he is done," the Vizier complained. The Princess's entourage encompassed as many shades of brown skin as the rainbow rocks of the Belit Gorge.

In the south, along the sea coast and in the trading ports, it had been easier. People were used to seeing foreigners. The farther north and deeper inland, the more a spectacle they made. For the most part they encountered only honest curiosity like the boy's.

"I suppose you want to send him a token, too," Vizier Hamandir grumped.

"Yes. Send him one of the mystic artifacts. Perhaps the gold bracers which ward off magic."

Hamandir's eyes opened wide in horror. Then his lips disappeared into a thin unamused line.

Aminira smiled serenely. "A wooden practice scimitar if we have one. Bow and arrows if we don't."

Another sigh rattled out of the Vizier as he called over a servant.

They were silent a time. Princess Aminira waved and smiled what she called the Royal Smile. It was set firm on her face. Friendly but not too friendly, pleasant but giving nothing away. With a nudge she made the Vizier wave too, but he only smiled at the pretty maidens they passed.

"Rather exotic, these milk-pale girls," the Princess observed slyly.

The Vizier's smile tightened into a grim line. "No. They are ignorant barbarians." He reached into his saddle bag and pulled out a cylindrical map case. The map inside, purchased two kingdoms ago from a cartographer the king swore by, unfurled across the pummel of his saddle. "This map is all wrong. The measurements little more than guesses. Even their most educated people are not worthy to be students in the University of Al Zahra."

"When you are done complaining, tell me where we are."

"According to this, we should be in Lagobel by now."

"Then we are close."

"We are also in luck. The first major city is the capitol

and it is a small country. We have little chance of getting lost. The King has a large castle on the shores of a lake. The city is supposedly very pleasant."

"Lucky indeed." Princess Aminira snatched the map from Vizier Hamandir and rolled it up. "Bring me Rana," she called out. A second later, a servant materialized beside her horse carrying a perch on which, hooded and tethered, sat her favorite hunting hawk. The servant handed her a thick leather glove and she slipped it on. She took the hawk from his perch, his weight settling on her hand. Even through the gloves she felt the power of his talons.

"Rana and I could use some exercise. I will wait for you further along the road."

The Vizier's face pinched in further displeasure but he said nothing. He waved at company of horse guards to follow. They broke from their column but before they could form up, Aminira spurred her horse to gallop. There was a gasp of awe from the peasants as she galloped away, the purple plume of her turban brooch caught the wind and the gold embroidery of her coat flashed in the sun. She was tempted to draw her scimitar and flourish it, but left her sword sheathed. It was enough that the scabbard sparkled with jewels. She didn't want to scare them. Just give them a pleasant memory they could look back on in later years and embellish.

She rode through the midst of the guards, startling their horses, and they were forced to scatter. She was to the tree line before they could recover. Behind her, the guards' horses whinnied their disgust. Then the sounds were swallowed by the forest as deep green pine boughs closed over her head, thick as roof beams, and greener than anything in her own country. The shadows beneath the canopy were cool and she was grateful for her gold embroidered surcoat. Summer in these northern countries was colder than winter in her own.

In a clearing she pulled her horse to a stop, waiting to see if her guards would catch up. They were used to this game and she won about half the time. Her hawk let out a piercing cry and Princess Aminira took off his hood. Rana blinked and shook out his grey and black striped feathers. She whistled softly to him, glad to be so far from home so she could fly the hawk without comment from the court ladies who mocked her manly pastimes.

Minutes passed and Aminira heard no signs of pursuit. She was alone in the silent forest. She'd lost the guards, or they'd lost her. Her breath eased out and it was as if she breathed for the first time in her life.

"Free," Aminira said to her hawk and her mare and the trees. These moments of utter aloneness, however brief they were, were unique in all her life. Back home, she was constantly attended, always watched, by the court, by servants, by her father and her uncle. "Free," she whispered again, trying to convince herself. As if the word alone could lift the burdens from her heart. It could not. When her father let her go he knew as well as she, that while she would never come home, she was still his daughter to command.

The shame of her cowardice could not be put off with mere words. Half an hour later Princess Aminira passed from shadow into light. A grassy meadow spread before her. Rana perked up at the sight of so much open space and sky. She launched him into the air and marveled at his speed. In seconds he was a dot against an expanse of blue.

Eyes closed, Aminira turned her face to the sun in longing, offering a prayer to the One God, May His Sun

Grant All Bounty, for the safety of her father and uncle. It was the only thing she could do now to assuage her guilt. Short of going home and facing the rising threat of a palace coup which would leave one of her dearest loved ones dead. The unbending laws of her country were harsh and unyielding in matters of succession. Her freedom was as illusory as Rana's. The hawk could soar in the sky until called back to be hooded and put away again in his travel cage.

Her father had ordered her to find a worthy prince to marry. It was the price for leaving, for begging out of the brewing storm in her palace home. She could never shame him more by disappearing into the wilderness. She opened her eyes, taking in the blue expanse dotted with fluffy white clouds, so unlike the brutal sky of the desert. The gentle sun and the lush greenery lulled her. She could almost feel herself growing soft and dull. How easy it would be to slip away and live in some emerald mountain valley, tending sheep in anonymity for the rest of her days. The weakness of such a thought almost angered her. She was stronger than such fantasies. Raised as a warrior, adept at court intrigue. And yet, she had still left. Aminira swallowed and turned her horse toward the forest as she turned away from her thoughts.

Vizier Hamandir bemoaned her pickiness each time they left a kingdom. They had been through a dozen in the last six months and each time Aminira found the princes wanting. The last one was a skinny arrogant horse-faced man with the straggling beard of a goat. He was five years older than she and his sole interest was in the ox carts of gold her caravan carried.

Hamandir said love didn't matter. He was a member

of the Deshari tribe and his female relatives had arranged his marriages to suit themselves. He had three wives and fifteen children he'd gladly left behind in Qadarh. Love may not be a requirement but rapport and respect needed to be present. She wanted to find some mutuality of feeling. Someone who didn't look at her and see a sack of gold coins.

High above the tiny pinprick of Rana wheeled in the gentle sky. She'd need to leave soon. The plan was to reach Lagobel by night fall then leave as swiftly as possible.

According to the King, Queen, and Prince of the last kingdom, the prince of Lagobel was under a curse. They weren't sure what the curse was, each said something different. He had been turned into a fish and never left the lake. He was too ugly to be let out of the castle. He was insane.

Hamandir listened to them seriously and determined that nothing more than a resupply stop was needed. They could present themselves to the king and queen as a matter of courtesy but there was no need for Aminira to meet the prince. She agreed, especially after a dozen disappointments by non-cursed princes.

Rana dove, she saw him target something on the far side of the meadow. The hawk was used to hunting in the desert scrub of Qadarh and he hadn't been as successful in these lands which had such abundant foliage. But he had been learning. Last time Princess Aminira had taken him hunting he'd come back with a tiny rodent she'd let him eat. Perhaps this time he would be back with something for the stewpot.

High green and yellow grasses waved as Rana fought his prey. He emerged with something large in his talons.

Aminira smiled a little, pleased at his success.

Rana flew toward her and she held out her gloved hand. He had a rabbit, fine and plump, fed on forest plants, fatter and juicier than the thin desert hares he normally caught.

The Princess climbed off her horse and put Rana on the saddle. She picked up the rabbit he had dropped at her feet and pulled a small dagger from the silken sash around her waist. She cut the eyeballs from the rabbit's head and gave them to the hawk as his reward for the hunt. When she got back to the caravan he would also receive the internal organs. Rana ate with relish, his beak, which could have easily ripped off her fingers, delicately took each eyeball from her bare palm.

With a bit of string she dug from her saddle bag, she tied the hind legs of the rabbit together and hung it from the pummel of the saddle. She put the hood back on Rana and remounted.

Like Rana, she was trained to return.

The sun lowered in the sky, dipping below the tree tops and creating a premature twilight. Aminira went an hour in what she thought was the right direction and didn't find the road. Without the sun she was lost.

She consulted the ill-drawn map. The biggest landmark was the lake to the north. If Aminira could find north, she'd be sure to reach the lake and could follow the shore to Lagobel castle. Her stomach growled, reminding her it was dinner time. Aminira sighed. She could keep riding in different directions and hope one of them was the right one, or she could stop for dinner and try to get her bearings.

Aminira slid off the horse and made a small camp. She built a fire and hung the rabbit from a low branch. Once gutted, she gave Rana the best of the internal organs, heart, liver, and lungs as a prize for his kill. She skinned the rabbit and fixed it as best she could to a wooden stake. A plain meal of roasted game. She was sorry not to have any spices with her but she hadn't planned on getting lost. Not that she knew how to use them in the first place.

When hunting with her father they had brought cooks with them. The desert hare and wild gazelle were handed off to a small army of servants who roasted and boiled the game to perfection.

Her stomach rumbled as she bit into the rabbit. The legs were burnt black and crispy, but the inside was perfect. No matter that the food was plain and overdone, she'd cooked it herself and a swell of pride made her smile genuinely for the first time in a long while.

After the small meal she doused the fire with dirt, keeping one dim smoky brand to light her way. Aminira led her horse by the reins and let Rana have the saddle. All she needed was a clearing to find the North Star and she'd know which direction to go.

Vizier Hamandir must be beside himself by now. No doubt search parties prowled the woods like aged hounds slow and steady in the darkness.

The trees thinned and high above shone a nearly full moon, flattened on one side but showering down silvery, flat grey light.

She found the North Star immediately. Another thing her father taught her, how to find her way by the stars. Even better, below the North Star, shimmering like a mirage, the lake glittered through the tree branches. Her eyes widened.

The sight was beautiful. The lake's black waters threw the moon's light back. The shore stretched across the distance, broken by hills and the faint silhouette of more pine forest.

At least the trees thinned from here onward. Chopped down for boats and fuel and homes. Princess Aminira fixed her position by the stars and struck off toward the lake.

CHAPTER 2

The lake shore was rockier than Aminira thought it looked from a distance. She walked with her night-blind mare on her right and a boulder strewn drop off to her left. The land rose and fell, marked by turns, sharp cliffs that rose from the water, and gentle rocky beaches paved with pebbles. The shore went on and on, curving in and out for miles. Across the still waters the lights of Lagobel castle and the city glowed like fairy lights. Dim but constant, and tantalizingly far away.

An hour later, just as the smoky fire brand was guttering, Aminira climbed a sharp hill and saw Lagobel castle, seemingly close enough to touch the lights in the windows. Behind her the dark abyss of the forest pressed at her back. This should be a lesson not to ride off again but she would not learn it. This was the only moment of peace she'd had in weeks.

A familiar fantasy came to her. She could run off, become a peasant and raise goats alone on a mountain top where no one knew her. The very idea shamed her and she squashed the vision. She refused to listen to her traitorous heart when it spoke to her of deeper freedoms she'd never considered before. Such a shame she could never live with. Already she had left behind too much to gain what freedom she had. She couldn't live without her honor as well.

Exhausted, Aminira tied her horse to a tree. She was too tired to press on to the castle. It wouldn't do to turn up like a vagabond in the night, alone and bedraggled. The poor mare was as tired as she was. The spongy ground beneath her feet was soft with grazing grass. They could both use some much needed rest and first thing in the morning she could go into town and see if her entourage had arrived.

A scream cut through the thick syrupy silence of the night. Startled, Aminira drew her scimitar. The sound came from the lake and she heard a splash followed by another shriek. Someone must be drowning.

She ran down the hill until she hit the stony beach. A pale figure, alone in the black waters of the lake could be seen a few dozen feet from shore, splashing in desperation. She threw down her sword and unbuckled the scabbard as she kicked off her shoes. Aminira stripped off her coat, turban, and vest as she dived into the water, leaving the clothing on the shore.

Her father had insisted she learn to swim in case she was ever to set foot on a boat. When she was ten he had thrown her off the royal barge into the silt brown waters of the River Elu. She had learned to swim that day and to never trust her father's teaching methods again. Now she was silently thankful.

The water dragged on her remaining clothing, a cotton dress over voluminous pants, but she reached the person screaming the lake water.

"Hang on," the Princess cried out as she reached through the darkness and looped her arm around what felt like a neck.

The person shrieked and went under dragging Aminira beneath the surface. She felt around blindly and tugged hard on the drowning victim's head and arm.

They surfaced and she coughed out a mouthful of earthy tasting lake water. Aminira kicked for shore, pulling the still panicking, half drowned person with her, skinny arms and legs alternately helped, hindered and kicked her.

In the shallows, she stood and scooped the now weakened drowning victim out of the water, cradling them like a child.

At last she looked down to see who she had rescued. Her mouth opened in surprise and her muscles froze in shock.

She held in her arms a young man. He was around her age, perhaps twenty or so. Burning Sun of Punishment she was touching a man! The warmth of his body seeped into her arms where her skin met his. It was forbidden for her to touch any man but blood relations and her husband. Her head was immodestly bare, the short tight curls of her hair dripped water into her eyes. Her coat and vest lay on the beach a few feet away. She was practically naked. And he was naked. From the waist up, moonlight caught the water that beaded across his bare chest. His slender frame, rangy muscle stretched over the bone like a hunting hound, weighed nothing in her arms.

But that wasn't right. How could Aminira stand on a beach holding a full grown, rather handsome, man in her arms? She should stagger under his weight.

Testing a theory, Aminira let go of him. He didn't fall.

He hung in the air, light as a spirit. She touched him again. His skin was warm and solid. As real and alive as she was.

He also yelled at her. "What do you think you're doing?" he demanded, mirth ringing in his voice as if he couldn't take his anger seriously. "Do you know who I am? I'm the Prince of Lagobel and you will put me back up into the lake!" Hysterical peals of laughter rang out over the waters.

Princess Aminira gasped and shoved the prince away. She had made a horrible mistake. He hadn't been a drowning victim screaming for help. He had been laughing.

The prince shifted and spun lazily in the air, long legs, covered in soggy breeches, stretched out but didn't reach the ground. Embarrassment aside, Aminira looked up and tried not to stare but it was impossible not to.

He floated unsteadily in space like a feather. And with a new sort of warmth spreading in her chest, Aminira took in the prince's crooked grin, straight nose, and sharp cheek bones carved in silver light.

"The lake," he said and held out a hand to her, grin dissolving into manic giggles. "Put me back up before anything more happens."

Up? Perhaps his dialect had thrown her off. Surely he meant down or into. Her arms stayed firmly over her chest, torn between modesty and the desire to reach out and take his very forbidden hand.

"Before what happens?" She stalled. Long elegant tapered fingers reached out to her. His hands looked musical and she wondered if he played an instrument. They appeared smooth. Hers were rough with archery calluses.

A breeze blew from the lake and seeped through her wet clothes, chilling her to the bone. Aminira shivered, wishing she were not so foolish, wishing she was a bold northern girl who could no doubt take the prince's hand without thought.

"Before this happens." The prince laughed as the breeze picked him up like a stray leaf and blew him toward the tree tops.

Princess Aminira watched, stunned and unmoving longer than she should have. Only the shriek of his laughter moved her; it almost sounded like a cry for help.

Her turban. She ran across the pebbled beach and scooped it up, tearing off the jeweled and feather brooch securing it. Yards and yards of ivory silk unwound in her hands. Running back to the Prince, she searched for one end of the silk.

To her relief, the prince had caught the top of a young pine tree. He clung to the slender bough, feet angled to the stars. In a dizzy moment of misperception it looked as if the Prince hung precariously over an abyss clinging to a rope. He could be lost so easily, plunged into the sky and carried away forever on the winds.

Aminira's hands worked faster. She found the end of the turban and picked up a smooth stone from the shore. Then she tied the rock in silk and let out its considerable length.

"Hold on, Your Highness," she called.

The prince snorted and giggled. "That was the general plan."

She spun the weighted end of the turban to build momentum then released it, keeping a firm hold of the opposite end. Her aim was fair. The end of the turban caught in a branch a few feet shy of the prince.

"Good enough," he said and pulled himself hand over hand down the tree. He wrapped the end of the turban around his wrist. "Now, reel me in," he called. "Or, even better, fly me like a kite. Father refuses too."

Aminira's eyes widened, the very idea horrified her.

The prince shrieked with laughter again, shaking the tree top. "What a funny face!" he said when he could speak again.

"Funny?" Princess Aminira frowned. "None of this is funny. What is wrong with you?"

"I've lost my gravity," the Prince said. He pushed off against the tree and floated above Aminira, tethered to the earth only by the strand of silk and her hand. Another breeze swept by and he swayed with the air currents.

Quickly, Aminira reeled him in, his second suggestion too awful to contemplate. He didn't seem to know or care about the danger he was in.

She pulled him back to earth and he grabbed her shoulder to steady himself. Princess Aminira stiffened. There was nothing in the touch other than the fact the prince wobbled in the breeze and needed to hold something with gravity. The casual intimacy shocked her but she forced herself to relax despite her racing heart.

"Now you can fix your mistake," he grinned. This close she saw his face unlined by care or worry. Hers was unworn as well though, kept in a carefully blank mask perfected by years of practice.

The prince waited, his hand a glowing ember on her shoulder. His body heat passed through the cotton of her blouse. Fleeting as a half glimpsed bird, something like annoyance crossed his features but it was gone even before forming. The emotion and expression lost to another chuckle.

"Well?" he said. "Put me up into the lake."

Aminira looked him over and noticed for the first time

he was tall even without his feet on the ground. Again he used up. Perhaps he was deranged as the rumors she'd heard. "Umm," was the only sound she could manage.

"Just pick me up and put me in the water," the prince waved his arm, the movement making him bob in the air.

Desperate to keep him from floating away, Aminira grabbed his hand. She ran to the lake shore tugging the prince through the air like a streamer.

She waded into the lake up to her knees. "Will this do, Your Highness?"

Smiling wide and using Aminira for leverage, the prince swung his legs down. The instant his feet touched the water he sank. He let go of her hand, which went cold with the absence. The prince waded in until he was waist deep, then let himself fall back in the water to float.

Princess Aminira watched him as he paddled lazily about. He was different in the water. His face relaxed. The spasms of laughter calmed; was he more or less himself in the water? And without gravity, who was he?

She spotted a rock breaking through the calm surface of the waters not far from where the Prince swam. Aminira walked out to it and climbed onto the solitary island.

"Your face is funny," the prince said as he swam to her. He mimicked her serious expression and giggled. "My father looks like that all the time."

She nodded, understanding a little what must be the king's daily existence.

"I don't know what that face is," the prince continued. "Father and Mother say things like 'they worry' or 'they're 'afraid' but I have no idea what they mean."

Everything he said came with a blithe smile or honest grin followed by laughter of some sort. No gravity. She pondered the implications even as she watched him, her eyes half lidded so as not to seem impertinent. He did not yet know she was a princess and for the moment, she didn't mind. Not that such information would change his demeanor at all.

No gravity...No grave emotions. No fear or pain, sorrow or worry, no gnawing empty questions like, does my father love me?

Wild and ferocious envy bloomed in her heart so sudden that Aminira clutched the fabric of her blouse.

Could his lack of gravity also mean he lacked finer feelings? No soft, tenuous mixed emotions. The silken sweetness of longing. The joyful sorrow of remembering something about your deceased mother, may God keep her, you'd forgotten for years. No doubt love was lost to the prince as well. Love and hurt lived in the same breath.

She smiled at the prince. "Is this better?"

"Much." He smiled back and she thought it his most genuine yet. "I haven't introduced myself. I am his royal highness, Prince Eadmund of Lagobel." He couldn't get through his title without giggling. "And you are?"

"Aminira Elamalesha," she said.

"Well, that's unique."

"Where I come from we would say the same of you."

"Really? How delightful."

"Yes. You're pale as desert sand."

The prince stood up in waist deep water and examined his arms with a look close to seriousness. "I'm actually much more tan since I spend all my time in the lake. You just can't tell in the moonlight"

"All your time?"

"Yes. It's the only place I get to be alone. After losing

me one too many times, Father decreed I must be tied to a dozen silk ropes held by a dozen courtiers if I want to go about on land."

"I can see why," Aminira said with a shiver, having nearly lost the prince to an errant breeze.

"But in the lake I'm on solid ground and cannot blow away."

She lay back on the wide, flat rock and thought about his odd expression 'put up into' the lake. If constantly threatened with falling off the Earth she could see why the lake might be considered 'up' and the whole world 'down'.

"You don't sleep in the lake, surely?" she asked.

"No. I'll go in for some sleep in a few more hours. See that tower? With the balcony?"

Aminira sat up and saw which one he pointed to. "Yes, I see."

"That's my bedroom. You know what you should do?"

"What?" Princess Aminira asked, mildly alarmed he would suggest anything involving his bedroom.

"Throw me down out of the water until I land on the underside of the balcony. No one will be able to find me for hours! Days! It'll be the greatest fun!" He laughed.

"That's horrible," Princess Aminira gasped. "I will not. And you should know better than to think it funny."

"There's that silly face again," he guffawed so hard he fell back into the water.

He was delighted. She was irritated. What a reckless curse he was under.

"I will not help you scare people," Aminira said and lay back down. Her clothes were nearly dry and she was tired now that the shock of meeting the prince was over.

She looked up at the stars. They seemed farther away

than at home. The endless vault of sky stretched to the edge of the world in the desert. Here mountains blocked out the horizon, forests obstructed the view.

The prince's screaming laughter merged with the soft lapping of gentle waves against the shore. In a minute she would climb off the rock and wade back into the water. She needed to put some more clothes on. Though the prince seemed not to care or notice her disheveled state. Rana and her steady mare were waiting for her too. Why was there always so much to think about? Propriety. Duty. Honor. Their weight pressed her eyes shut. She just needed a moment to forget everything.

Her breathing relaxed and her last thought was her unwound turban still lying in the grass.

CHAPTER 3

Princess Aminira woke stiff and cold on the rock in the lake. The rock she lay on radiated a deep chill that numbed her bones until her whole body ached. She had not meant to fall asleep last night. Where was the prince? Could he see her? The clear morning air brought no sounds to her. The prince was gone. The only splashing she heard were fish catching insects. His laughter was gone too. Perhaps he'd finally gone home. Perhaps he clung to the underside of the balcony and the Palace was in an uproar searching for the missing prince. Aminira smiled, and then quickly stifled it. It was a cruel prank, funny, but cruel. His parents must worry unending about a son that could blow away like dust on the wind.

She stretched, groaned with pain as her joints popped in protest, and forced herself up. The sun was just above the distant mountain range, edging the peaks with summer gold. Already the air had warmed though not enough to warm Aminira.

For a moment she sat, massaging the feeling back into her limbs. She looked into the calm tea brown water of the lake. She could see the shallow bottom of rocks and pebbles.

Unhappy to get wet yet again, Aminira waded back to shore and collected her strewn belongings. She took the rock from her turban and loosely draped the battered silk over her head, turning it into a flowing scarf. Modesty forbade her going about in public with a bare head. Though the northern women did so all the time, Aminira couldn't quite bring herself to try it. Scandalous enough that the prince had seen her so immodest last night. She pinned the folds of fabric with the brooch, which would need a new feather after last night. Further along the beach she found her shoes, grateful to put some leather between her feet and the rocky beach.

Once on the grass, she knelt in prayer to Re-Hurakh the One God singing the prescribed words of the cant to the east, thanking Him for the new day and for the night passed in safety. Twice a day, prayers were offered to the God's Bountiful Sun, morning and evening, in thanks for each day lived on earth.

Backtracking along the rugged shore, Aminira came to her horse and hawk. She led the horse to the lake so the mare could drink. She unhooded Rana and let him fly. He circled overhead a few times then landed and drank his fill. When he was done, she called him back and returned the hood. He was a young hawk and still nervous in crowds, and Aminira was going straight to the city of Lagobel.

She had decided to stay.

Vizier Hamandir would not be happy but something about the prince intrigued her. She would find her entourage, introduce herself to the king and queen and gain a formal introduction to Prince Eadmund. She wanted to find out more about him and his curse.

Aminira mounted her horse and winced as her lower back twinged. The woods, the lake, and the distant city were splendid in the morning air, fantastical in their unfamiliarity and full of promise.

As she rode, the sun rose higher, banishing the shadow of the mountains. The air shimmered promising, what to these Northern climes, would constitute a hot day. The lake shore smoothed and Aminira turned inland onto a wide gravel road that crunched with her horse's every footstep. The road curved away from the palace and toward the city through farms and parkland. Soon the gravel road ended and Aminira found herself on a stone paved track worn by cartwheels and heavy traffic. She was back in civilization again.

People and animals passed to and from the city, the people eyeing her openly or suspiciously; the animals indifferent. Some people smiled and waved to everyone they passed, Aminira being no exception. She greeted them all the same, giving them the Royal Smile. She waved and nodded and smiled her way into the city.

Inside the gates the streets were packed with more people and animals jostling for space on the road. There were riders on horseback like herself, carts of vegetables on their way to market, and herds of pigs, chickens, and sheep on their way to sale or slaughter.

Street vendors shouted, trying to sell her food, drink, trinkets, or a room for the night. Aminira kept riding, unsure where she was going. Vizier Hamandir would have the guards searching for her but she could see no one she knew. She must have missed them somehow. They could still be in the woods scouring the countryside, fearful she was lost in the woods.

The Vizier enjoyed his luxuries. In every city they'd visited he chose the finest inn for the first night's stay. After that they were often invited to stay in the palace or given the run of some noble's estate for the duration of their visit.

This was the first time she'd ever had to find an inn on her own. Aminira stuck to the widest avenues hoping she would happen upon wherever her caravan was staying. Not much of a plan. She needed to ask someone for help.

Aminira looked around and saw a filthy little lump of rags jump up from the corner of a doorway. A girl, thin and small of indeterminate age, ran straight for Aminira, eyes wide and shining.

"Mistress, are you with the foreigners who arrived yesterday?"

Aminira tugged her mare to a halt. "Yes, I am. Do you know where they are staying?"

The girl smiled showing a mouth full of crooked teeth. Her ruddy complexion turned crimson with enthusiasm. "I do, I do. The Lemon Balm Inn on Fir Street. It's the biggest inn there is. Five stories high." She held up four fingers then corrected herself and put out her thumb. "Five," she repeated.

The girl's hand was caked in dirt and Princess Aminira's nose wrinkled as she caught a whiff of the urchin. The rags she wore might once have been a dress but no longer

"Lead me to the inn and I'll have the kitchen give you a meal."

The girl nodded so hard her head looked in danger of flying off. "This way." She trotted up the street, bare feet flapping on the paving stones.

Aminira clicked her tongue to get her mare moving. She caught up to the girl easily and said, "Tell me, girl, what do you know of Lagobel's Prince Eadmund?"

"He's cursed," she said. "People call him the Light Prince 'cause he's light as a feather not on account of being shiny. The king's none too pleased with him. People in the market bellyache all the time 'bout the King has no heir."

So Aminira did have something in common with Prince Eadmund. She was not her father's heir, nor was he. With his curse there was no way the Prince could rule, and she was unaccountably glad to have something in common with him.

Her guide pointed right at the next wide intersection lined with thick old trees. "This way," the girl said turning onto the street. "So all them people you with foreigners?" she asked.

"Yes. We come from the Sultanate of Qadarh. A great country across the Tamis Sea and far to the south." Aminira hadn't enjoyed the two months of slow ship travel confined in such small quarters, but she was grateful enough to be in a new place with new sights and new people.

"What's the funny looking humpy animals you got?"

"They are called camels."

"Can I pet one?"

"You can try. They are mean animals. Ornery at the best of times. It may try to bite you," Aminira answered honestly. She had never gotten along with the cantankerous beasts and preferred horses.

"I still want to," the girl said, chin jutted with determination.

Princess Aminira hid her smile behind her hand. "The

camels will be stabled with our other beasts."

"Good." The girl nodded and kept marching down the street, forced to stick close to Aminira's mare by the city bustle. Heavy carts and swift carriages dodged each other. Street sweepers swept, maids washed the steps of fine stone houses, bakery and milk carts stopped at their appointed rounds.

"Tell me, girl, have you ever seen the prince?" Last night felt like a vivid waking dream. She could have made it all up. Eadmund laughing so hard at her serious face, his hands, warmer than the summer night. He'd smelled of lake water and pine when she'd fished him out of the sky. What if somehow she'd made it all up, and like a cloud, he dissipated in the sun.

"No. I never seen the prince. He's not in the parades the king is in," the girl said. "And my name's Bea. What's yours?"

"A pleasure to meet you, Bea. My apologies. I am Aminira." Her manners were slipping. Instead of pondering the prince and his infectious smile she should have asked the girl's name and given her own.

"There, that's the Lemon Balm." Bea waved her crusty finger at a tall peaked roofed building. The inn was newer than its neighbors and painted jaunty yellow. Lemon trees in planters lined the wide stairs. It certainly looked expensive enough for Hamandir. Despite the luxuries the poor man was probably out of mind with worry.

"Can you show me to the stables, Bea?" she asked, wanting to see her horse and Rana taken care of before having to listen to Hamandir's disapproving lecture on not riding off on her own again.

"Round back," Bea said. She led Aminira around the

block to a wide alley covered with an arch. Beyond the open gates was the inn's coach yard. A wide square courtyard framed by bales of hay piled along one wall, the inn's plain stone back, unpainted like the facade, and generous stable forming the third wall. The back of an unknown building created the alley they had come down.

The ranks of the inn's servants, dressed in yellow livery, were swollen by her own servants in their desert robes. When they saw their princess they rushed over bowing and laughing with relief. She saw the wagon master send one of the grooms into the inn no doubt to fetch the Vizier.

"Your Highness, we're so glad to have you back safe. Praise Re-Hurakh," The wagon master bowed deeply.

"Please, I'm fine," Aminira said. She dismounted and handed the reins of her mare over to a servant. He led the mare and hawk away to the stable.

"You're a princess?" Bea stood with rigid shock, eyes so wide Aminira could see the whites all the way around.

Aminira smiled what she called her 'beneficent' smile, wider than the bland Royal Smile, and added a wink. "My full name is Princess Aminira Eshenya Elamalesha. But Aminira is fine."

"It is not," the wagon master sputtered. He pushed Bea's head down, forcing her into a bow. "Show respect."

"As you will show my kindly guide respect," Aminira said to the wagon master, an edge of steel creeping into her voice.

The wagon master took the hint and let Bea go. He bowed again and kept his eyes on the cobble stones of the courtyard. Bea's head popped up like a cork on water and she went right back to staring open-mouthed at Aminira.

"This little girl is Bea and she was kind enough to show

a stranger around the city."

Bea's dirty hands knotted together, "Begging pardon mistress–Your Highness, I'm thirteen or so... Not a little girl."

The girl was so small. She must never have had a full meal her whole life. Aminira bit down on a frown. There were children just like her on every street back home. Some things didn't change from place to place, land to land. Though she wished such tragedies were not so common.

"Very good then young lady, you have my gratitude." Aminira turned to the wagon master. "Without her I would not have known where the caravan was quartered. Order her the finest meal the Lemon Balm Inn has to offer and after that ready a camel. Bea would like to ride one."

"Yes, Your Highness." The wagon master bowed twice more then went to speak to the grooms.

"Go with him." Aminira gestured at Bea. The girl's body swiveled in the direction the wagon master had gone but her eyes remained fixed on Aminira. At last Bea turned her head and trotted toward the stables.

The back door of the inn crashed open and Vizier Hamandir's dark brown eyes swept over the courtyard. His shocked gaze settled on Aminira. The servants must have just woken him, his curly grey hair was pulled into a knot behind his head and he was still in his long white night shirt with a robe thrown carelessly over it.

"Princess Aminira, where have you been?" he shouted over the courtyard. Like a raging djinn he ran down the steps of the inn, fear and relief warred over his lined face. "Thank Merciful God you are safe," he covered his face with his hands, kissed them and raised them to the sky, giving thanks to Re-Hurakh. "I had men searching the woods all night. There are still parties out there! How could we have missed you? I beg you, have mercy on an old man and be more responsible. If anything had happened to you it would be my head. Do you understand?" he bellowed even as he bowed low.

Perhaps the search parties which had missed her, were turned aside by fate. Perhaps Divine Providence had intended for her to meet the cursed prince. Were they destined for each other? The thought brought a smile to her face and she hid it with a bow to Hamandir. "I am sorry. I was lost in the woods. I made my way to the lake but it was too late to continue on. I slept there and left at dawn."

The black smudges around his eyes and grey cast to the Vizier's bronze skin spoke more than his words. She had known the Vizier almost her whole life and knew a good portion of his concern was not just for his head, but for her.

Hamandir's face softened. "You will not leave without an escort again," he said. "We cannot risk losing you in these barbarous lands."

"Fear not, Vizier. We shall be staying in Lagobel awhile."

"We agreed to a resupply stop," he said, surprised.

"This is a charming country." With a charming prince, thought Aminira. She felt a touch of heat rise in her cheeks. "I would like to see more of it," she added as casually as possible.

The Vizier's shock worked itself all the way down to annoyance till at last he gave another of his long suffering sighs. "Very well. I will send a messenger to the king and arrange to introduce ourselves." He looked over her dirty clothes and the ragged turban turned shawl. "If you wish to meet the king you should make yourself presentable. I had the inn set aside its finest rooms for you."

Hamandir snapped his fingers and servants, both theirs and the inn's, rushed to the summons. He recited a long list of instructions and at last Aminira was led upstairs by a maid in a cheery yellow uniform.

The suite reserved for her was on the fifth floor and Aminira was relieved when the maid threw open the gold and white double doors. The first room was a luxurious sitting room with glass doors the likes of which Aminira had never seen. Through the doors she saw a stone balcony with potted lavender. The summer breeze blew in from the balcony bringing the floral scent with it.

Her maids were waiting for her and they bowed to Aminira as she entered.

She was shown to the bedroom which had a closet big enough for all her trunks, a dressing room, and a private bathroom with a huge copper tub.

"Can you draw me a bath?" Aminira asked the maid.

"Of course, Your Highness." She curtsied and promptly disappeared.

While she waited for the succession of maids carrying steaming buckets of hot water with which to fill the tub, she ordered her lady's maid to unpack the fine formalwear buried in her luggage. As yet unused were sparkling gowns and vests, bodices embroidered with gold, voluminous silk pants worn under everything, velvet hats with lace veils, and a king's ransom in jewelry she hadn't worn since leaving home. There had been no one she cared to impress.

Until now.

Not that the prince would care about fine jewelry and cloth-of-gold, but she would feel prettier wearing such things. There was also a king and queen to impress. Nothing, in her experience, impressed a king quite so much as gold.

"Your bath is ready, Your Highness," said one of the inn's maids. She held an empty wooden bucket in her hand and bowed as she spoke.

Aminira nodded. "Thank you." The maid departed and she had her own servants leave her to bathe alone. She left off surveying her wardrobe.

The bathroom smelled pleasantly of citrus and lavender. Aminira leaned over the steaming copper tub as she stripped off her grubby travel clothes. Purple blossoms of lavender floated on the surface of the water and a square hunk of creamy yellow soap infused with lemon sat ready for use in a copper basket hung from the side of the tub.

She sank gratefully into the hot water. The heat soaked away the aches from a night spent sleeping on bare rock.

Aminira closed her eyes and breathed in the bright lemon lavender scent. Prince Eadmund swam into her daydreams unbidden. Perhaps, at this very moment, he was drifting in the waters of the lake. Maybe he slept in his tower bedroom, taking some rest at last. Hopefully he would be scaring no one today. A wide smile pulled at her lips, and, as there was no one there to see, she gave in and chuckled at the memory of the laughing prince.

CHAPTER 4

The royal retinue gathered in the courtyard of the Lemon Balm Inn. Princess Aminira watched the horses and guardsmen lineup. Near the stable, Bea stood with a camel petting its large soft nose. The girl should have gone home long since. Although, Aminira realized she probably had no home to go to.

Perhaps she'd like a job. Bea seemed to have a way with camels, no small skill, as the beasts never seemed to like anyone.

"Are we—" Vizier Hamandir grunted and stopped as he trotted down the courtyard steps. "I've not seen that outfit before. We're having an audience with the king not going to a ball."

Aminira felt her cheeks grow hot and she tugged the silk veils draped from her fez closer around her face. She felt the Vizier looking her over. An unasked question hung between them. What, or who, was she so dressed up for?

She wiped sweaty palms on her brocade sash, trying

to look like she was making sure her jeweled dagger was secure. Then pointed at Bea. "Look at the girl. We should offer her a job taking care of the camels." Aminira held her breath and hoped the Vizier would drop the subject of her outfit.

He looked across the yard, squinting in disapproval. Bea had grown even filthier during her short time in the stables.

Then the Vizier's eyebrows twitched in contained surprise. "If she can charm such a beast as a camel… I will send one of our grooms to her family and find out if they will part with her."

Princess Aminira silently let out her held breath. Even better, one of the inn's stable boys brought out the horse she was riding to the palace, a slender black mare with a gold bridle. The mare was spoiled and temperamental but she thrived on attention and made a good parade horse.

"Time to depart," Aminira said, eager to leave the conversation behind.

The ride to the palace was thankfully brief and Aminira didn't have to talk to the Vizier the entire way. She made a big show of waving to the people who gathered along their route to get a look at the foreigners in their exotic garb.

The palace turrets came into view, light blue stone trimmed in abundant creamy limestone carvings. The towers and crenellations became clear as they rode closer. Aminira tried to spot the Prince's tower but they all looked alike. She wondered what he kept in his rooms, what his interests were. Perhaps, without gravity, he couldn't truly appreciate art or literature.

Aminira and her entourage rode through the palace gates. Beyond was a wide road cut through a garden of short grass and sculpted hedges. A grand staircase wide enough to ride six horses up side-by-side lead to a grand portal sculpted with a bas-relief of the lake and the mountains beyond.

Pages in azure livery, carrying the flag of Lagobel, six gold stars on a lake of blue, lined the road. From on high, trumpets announced them. Small against the stonework of the castle, Princess Aminira saw the king and queen at the center of a cluster of nobles.

She did not see the prince. The heart drained out of her official smile and she became aware of the effort it took to smile so much, for so long. Her face hurt and she let her muscles relax.

When she reached the base of the steps Princess Aminira dismounted along with Vizier Hamandir. She bowed deeply to the waiting court.

Then Vizier Hamandir stepped forward and introduced her. "May I present, her royal highness, Princess Aminira Elamalesha, daughter of Sultan Caylim Elamalesha the second." His voice echoed off the stone walls of the palace and he bowed gracefully to the monarchs of Lagobel.

The King of Lagobel, a short, florid-faced man with a barrel chest and ample girth, looked them over with something akin to amused irritation.

"Yes, yes. We're very happy to receive you," the king said. "I'm King Luberto. This is my wife, Queen Gwinden." The king gestured to the gathered nobles behind him. "This lot is worthless. You'll meet them in due course I dare say..."

The nobles looked very carefully at anything but the king.

Princess Aminira bit her lower lip until her eyes watered

to stifle a surprised urge to laugh. She was appalled, or at least felt she ought to be, by the king's behavior. Back in her own country pomp and decorum were the watchwords by which all lived. Politeness etched in stone, followed to the letter lest offence be given. But this King Luberto threw everything she was familiar with out the window like the contents of a used chamber pot, and left the room fresher for it.

"We have prepared a luncheon on the lake shore for you." Queen Gwinden stepped forward and sharply elbowed her husband in the ribs on the way. "It is not every day we receive such elevated company as yourselves." She curtsied, not too low, just a bob to Princess Aminira.

"By all means let's get out of this blasted sun," the King said. He spun on his heels and shoved the nobles aside as he made for the castle's grand entryway.

The queen gave a rigid dazzling smile and said, "Please, follow me, Princess."

Vizier Hamandir looked at Aminira, one eyebrow raised, desperate with questions. His expertise in etiquette suddenly without use.

Aminira shrugged, then waved her hand in the direction the king had disappeared. Unless they wanted to stand about in the courtyard all day, they might as well follow the queen.

Hamandir glared his disapproval at yet more uncivilized behavior. Aminira was again tempted to laugh but she headed after Queen Gwinden. A second later she heard his footsteps behind her.

They followed the queen, who was paces behind her surly husband, followed by the troop of nobles who grumbled in low voices now that the king was out of earshot.

The palace was as lovely inside as out. Vaulted stone ceilings of carved lattice work soared overhead. Paintings and tapestries hung on the walls. Hunting scenes, portraits of past kings and even one hallway lined with nothing but paintings of horses. As they walked, too swiftly to take in much detail, Queen Gwinden promised a personal tour of the palace.

Aminira agreed, enthusiastic to see more at a leisurely pace. The Vizier agreed out of politeness. He had looked cross that an entire gallery should be nothing but horses, as though it were a waste of paint and canvas.

The seemingly endless vaulted hallways came to an end at a terrace overlooking a long expanse of gently sloping gardens that made their way to the lake.

"Beautiful," Aminira said as she at last caught up to the king.

He smiled. "Ought to be, they cost my grandfather enough."

"Beauty may have its price, but the joy it brings priceless," Aminira said.

The King let loose a chuckle. "Well, isn't that poetic?" He strode off down a wide paved path edged with fragrant roses, leaving everyone to hurry after.

A table waited for them on the lake shore laid with a feast. Sweet and savory scents mixed with the fresh lake air and garden blossoms. Bowls of fruit, plates of delicate pastries and meat pies, a barnyard's worth of roasted animals, accompanied by vegetables and silver pitchers of drinks.

"Your Majesty is too kind. This is a feast, not a luncheon," Aminira said.

"Nonsense." The king waved away her compliment. "I

like a good meal every fortnight—"

"Every week," Queen Gwinden cut in.

"Once in a while." The king glared at her. "It's just your good luck I like to invite interesting people, listen to them talk."

"Then mock them in private," the Queen muttered.

"What was that, my dear?" King Luberto asked, still glaring sternly at his wife.

"Nothing darling."

No one said anything for a second and in the silence dragonflies buzzed. Then the nobles covered their discomfort with court gossip and laughter. Everyone drifted into little circles of friends and conspirators. Queen Gwinden looped her arm around Aminira's elbow and guided her through the crowd, introducing a gaggle of lords and ladies, dukes and duchesses.

During the introductions, more guests drifted in. A pair of philosophers from far off Jiuzhou, an alchemist who wore a pristine white apron and gloves, and a group of doctors all in black, like a swarm of flies.

"Now we eat." King Luberto thumped the table, his voice easily carried over the party.

Everyone found their seats; each place was marked with a name card. The seats dictated both rank and what must be the king's whims. Aminira found herself seated on King Luberto's immediate right and next to her sat Vizier Hamandir. Across the table, sat the philosopher, alchemist, and doctors, then the nobles, all the way to Queen Gwinden, who sat at the other end of the table opposite her husband.

"So, leeches and sawbones, what have you to say about my son?" King Luberto asked as the servants dished out cold vegetables with a dressing of vinegar and spices.

Aminira sat straighter and listened attentively. This must be the true purpose of the lunch, to discuss the prince's accursed condition.

"Is the prince not joining us?" Aminira asked before the reports could begin.

"What? No," the king said. "Not unless we need an extra flag to fly. My son is afflicted with a curse. Not a deadly one, but deathly irritating nonetheless. These learned gentlemen are the latest vultures circling with the promise of a cure."

"I propose," said the alchemist, "injecting His Highness with gold. The injections along with a tonic of jade and mercury should adhere the gold to his bones thereby restoring his gravity."

Beside the princess, Vizier Hamandir snorted and coughed out a bite of food into his napkin. She knew his thought. The alchemist's suggestion was ludicrous and the only possible outcome would be the prince's death. Aminira looked to the king. Surely he would know better.

The king's face reddened, his grey blonde hair stood out, vivid against his complexion.

"I daresay," King Luberto pounded the table. The crystal and porcelain jumped then settled with a loud clatter. "Why don't you try that on yourself and get back to me, eh?"

The alchemist shrank in his seat and stroked his long beard nervously.

Aminira exhaled, relieved the king had such good sense. Back home unscrupulous chemists peddled such tonics and potions. Billed as cures to the unwary and the desperate, they often caused more harm than good. Aminira found herself liking this king in spite of, or perhaps because of, his utter rudeness. He spoke his mind and his feelings were obvious. The Sultan had always been a hard man for her to read. She respected her father's self-contained nature, learned from it well. That sort of inscrutableness was drilled into all the royal family, herself included. But it was hard to never know his feelings for anything, or if he even entertained them at all.

"Anyone else have any ideas? Hmm?" King Luberto looked over the table, eyes narrowed. He pointed at one of the doctors with a chicken leg. "You, what have you got?"

The doctor jumped and looked at the alchemist who had sunk so low in his seat only his hooked nose and busy eyebrows could be seen above the edge of the table.

The doctor wiped his brow with his napkin and cleared his throat. "My thought is that the prince's body is backwards. He is light where he should be heavy. The blood is sent forth by the veins and returns by the arteries. Consequently it runs through him the wrong way. Opposite every other living thing on earth. Seeing that such is the case, his gravitation also runs opposite. My proposal for a cure is this: Bleed him until he reaches the last point of safety. When His Highness is reduced to a state of perfect asphyxia, apply a ligature to the left ankle and the right wrist. Then attach air pumps to opposite hand and foot, inserting them into vein and artery—"

The king hurled the half eaten chicken leg at the doctor. It smacked the doctor in the face. Aimed dead between the eyes and thrown with enough force to throw the doctor off balance, he fell back into his chair with a grunt.

The king stood up and bellowed, "You're damned lucky I didn't throw a knife."

Princess Aminira looked at the Vizier from the corner

of her eye. He glanced back at her with a similar stony expression of shock. The princess was sure she had never been to a lunch quite like this in all her life.

"Have none of you anything that won't kill my son in the name of curing?" the King demanded.

There was a long silence while the remaining doctors and the two philosophers thought hard about saying anything. At last the elder philosopher elbowed the younger and he stood up quietly clearing his throat.

"Wu-Pei, what have you two cooked up?" Luberto asked as he picked up the sharpest knife from among his tableware.

The philosopher gulped and said, "We think perhaps that all His Highness needs do is cry. We have seen firsthand the effect that water has on Prince Eadmund. He is calmer, more thoughtful, and his gravity is normal. Tears are a grave matter, they come from the heart, which is the emotional center of the body. So, if the he were to shed a tear, we believe all his gravity would come back and the curse would be broken."

King Luberto grunted. "At least no one dies in your scenario. But it's impossible. The boy never shed a tear in his life. Not pain, not spankings, not spiders, nothing I've tried has ever got him to cry."

"I'm sorry, your majesty," Wu-Pei said. "It's just a theory. We'll work on it more." He bowed low, his head nearly touching the table top.

"Better than these other fools." the king looked pointedly at the doctor and the alchemist. "They can pack their belongings right now and get out of my kingdom by sunset or I shall inflict them with their own cures."

The two men jumped up from the table. The doctor

knocked over his chair in his haste and ran for the castle. The alchemist, old as he was, hobbled quickly after.

The king roared with laughter. The Queen sighed and said, "I'm glad they are gone, but honestly you could just dismiss them."

"Come now, you heard what they wanted to do to your son."

"Pardon me, Your Majesty," Aminira interjected before the conversation could turn, "but do you happen to know the exact circumstances of his Highness' curse?" She wanted to know if perhaps she could help in some way the king, queen and the doctors hadn't thought of yet. Her father had let her depart with a number of magical objects from the treasury. Though most of them for warding off magic. The Sultan didn't want Aminira to fall victim to foreign enchanters. But maybe something in her possession could cure Eadmund.

"We're fairly certain it was Luberto's sister," the queen's eyes narrowed at the king. "Princess Yisabelle. She cursed him on his naming day. Eadmund was born normal. He cried and had weight until then."

"There are no witnesses," he countered.

"Several people heard her chant something under her breath."

"None who will step forward in court," the King said sullenly and stared into his wine. He drained the glass and a servant rushed to fill it again.

"She wasn't invited to the naming ceremony but turned up anyway, despite the fact she was in deep mourning," Queen Gwinden continued, her voice rigid. "Her powers are well known."

The air over the lunch table curdled. The nobles and

the two remaining philosophers all looked uncomfortable, yet resigned. This was probably an old argument between the king and queen. One never resolved which surfaced periodically. This time it was Aminira's fault it had risen up.

"The law is the law. She is still of royal blood and there is no proof," the king said.

"My apologies, Your Majesty. I did not mean to bring up old hurts," Aminira said.

Queen Gwinden pushed away her plate of uneaten food and said, "I think lunch is over. Princess Aminira, it was lovely to meet you. We are preparing a fête in your honor. Invitations will be sent shortly."

Without waiting for a more formal dismissal the nobles excused themselves from the table, followed by the philosophers. The King grunted his good-byes and waved them away.

Aminira's food settled like a rock in stomach. She stood and pulled the Vizier up after her. She bowed low to the king and queen. "My deepest apologies. As a guest I should never have spoken so. I am not as ill-mannered as this, truly. I have shamed my father and my family. I will find a way to make this right. You have my word."

"Nonsense," the King said. "You asked an honest question, which is more than usually happens at this table."

Princess Aminira curtsied and the Vizier bowed. She hesitated to leave without more goodbyes and a more formal leave from the king. In Qadarh it was rude to leave a party even after the goodbyes. One should not look eager to go. But she was no longer at home and must do as bid by the King of Lagobel.

Aminira took the Vizier by the arm and steered him from the table. He bowed again and Aminira couldn't help another curtsy at the edge of the gardens. Only then could they turn and leave.

Halfway back to the castle Hamandir could remain silent no longer. Aminira saw his mouth and eyebrows working to contain his thoughts but in the shade of a trellis covered with fragrant white roses, he stopped and said, "Those are the rudest people I have met in my life. Are they insane?"

"No, I think they are just suffering."

"Why are we staying in this vulgar place? Jackals have more manners. Fleas, dogs, anything. This place is madness. Worse than all the others, and yet you insist on staying even after that travesty of a luncheon?" He pointed down the hill toward the lakeshore as if he could rub out the last hour with his finger if only he scrubbed at the view hard enough.

"Keep your voice down," Aminira ordered. "Would you shame me more?"

Vizier Hamandir grew sullen and quoted, "'No one is shamed before mongrels. You have nothing to make up for. If anything they should be crawling at your feet begging for forgiveness."

"Stop it. They are king and queen and we are guests in their country," Aminira said. "We leave when I say so and not before."

The Vizier shifted on his feet, obviously wanting to say more. She hoped he didn't. She didn't want to argue. Aminira stared her most imperious stare down her nose at Hamandir. He looked away at last pretending to notice the roses.

"Let us go back to the inn and await our invitation," Aminira said. She marched away, not waiting for a reply.

CHAPTER 5

The rocky lakeshore stretched out as silver as the flat of Princess Aminira's scimitar. She slid off her mare and listened for the sound of laughter.

Only the distant cry of a night bird echoed over the lake. Aminira forced her disappointment aside. Perhaps it was too early for the prince to be out swimming. He could be home sleeping like sensible people. Like she ought to be.

Aminira had recruited Bea to help her escape. Bea had gladly given Aminira directions to a short cut out of the city that would help her evade the night watch. Then helped pack her saddle bags and even suggested she could take Aminira's place in bed. Should a servant come in it would look like Aminira was sleeping. Aminira told her that wasn't necessary but thanked her for the suggestion. Bea seemed to have a head full of romantic notions and Aminira wondered where she had come by them. Of course the age of thirteen (or so) was the right age for such notions to take over and Aminira couldn't fault her.

Prepared to wait, Aminira lit a candle with flint and steel. She placed it in a lantern with amber glass panes, casting a warm glow across the stones. Tied across the back of her saddle was a small carpet. With a snap she unrolled it and laid it near the water's edge where the rocks thinned to pebbles. She added some pillows on top for cushioning. Much more comfortable, she settled in, hopeful he would come. Part of her whispered she was being foolish and he had probably forgotten her the instant she left his sight.

Why should he come? The lake was vast. Perhaps he swam the other direction tonight. Their meeting must have had little impact on him because of the curse. She was the one who desired to see him again though she tried desperately not to.

Aminira gazed up at the stars, all in slightly different positions than they were at home. She picked out her favorite constellations. The Jackal, the Scorpion, the Lovers. Every time she found one, she looked out over the water, watching for a pale dot.

She gave herself until the candle burned down to wait then she would leave and wait on the promised invitation from the king and queen. Surely they would introduce him to her eventually. It was only proper. Until then, she could wait on the shore.

An hour later, after she had given up hope, convinced herself she'd regret leaving, and grown hopeful once again, Aminira heard rhythmic splashing. She rushed to her feet and looked down the shore.

Prince Eadmund swam parallel to the beach. Each stroke churned the water into quicksilver under the moon's light. His laughter carried to Aminira's ears and she thought it sincerer than the night before.

Aminira waved her lantern, unaccustomed delight bubbling up in her. She toed off her silk slippers and took off her long coat. Beneath was an appropriate enough swimming costume. Blouse with elbow length sleeves and voluminous pants that belled out then gathered in a cuff buttoned just below her knees. Pinned around her head was a gauzy scarf covering the short, tight curls of her hair. Tonight, she could swim with the Prince and preserve her modesty. She shoved down the voice of her father which pointed out swimming with a young man after midnight was the very definition of immodesty.

"Hello!" Prince Eadmund called out as he swam closer. He laughed and said, "I'm glad you're here. I was hoping you would be."

Her heart swelled, but Aminira smoothly asked, "You are?"

The prince swam closer to shore and stood in waist-high water, as close as he could come without losing the weight the water gave him.

"Of course I'm glad." He grinned and pushed a dripping lock of hair off his forehead. "I'm always glad." He chuckled.

"Of course you are," Aminira said as her heart deflated. He would no doubt have been equally happy to see a camel.

"I have some mischief in mind." the prince guffawed and tapped the side of his head.

"Not that terrible balcony prank?" Aminira would never help him with that especially after meeting the thin, wan queen who'd eaten nothing at lunch.

"No, no, though I still think it's a grand idea."

Eadmund pointed to Aminira and laughed. "You look so silly. What is that face?"

She smoothed over her alarm and the prince gathered his few wits together.

"Follow me up that way." He pointed left. "There's something I'd like to show you."

He held his hand out, reaching across the water but she was too far away to touch. His enthusiastic smile decided it for Aminira. She waded into the cool water. Goosebumps prickled her flesh and she shivered.

The prince only laughed. "Come on, hurry up. The sooner you dive in the faster you'll be used to the temperature. Look at me."

Look at him indeed. Aminira felt her entire body flush with heat. Prince Eadmund wore his usual swimming breeches, and nothing else. She dove into the water, extinguishing the heat inside her in a single tidal chill. She surfaced a few feet from him and said. "Let's go."

He didn't need further encouragement. With a whoop of laughter Eadmund dove into the water and was off.

Aminira followed; glad he stayed parallel to the shore. There was no way she could keep up with him, no human being could. Even if she shed her swim clothes, which dragged on her in the water, she could not have caught him.

Far ahead, Aminira saw the Prince turn, as if to speak to someone, noticed he was alone, and swim back to her.

"I suppose most people don't swim as fast as I do," he said as he circled her in the water.

"Great blue fish don't swim as fast as you," Aminira said. "Can I just walk?" She paused and tread water to get her breath back.

"I have a better idea," Prince Eadmund grinned, his eyes flashed in the moonlight. What color were his eyes? Blue? Gray? Silver? Impossible to tell at night. Aminira wanted to know.

He swam until he was right in front of her then spun around in the water, presenting his back to her.

"Hold on to me. I can swim us both there."

The greedy water leeched away the warmth of Princes Aminira's hot blush. The prince had no idea what he was asking. She took a deep breath. He didn't care either. She could be anyone or anything. All were equally amusing in his eyes. And if he didn't care, she shouldn't either.

Aminira wrapped her arms around his neck, careful not to choke him. Her body molded to his and her face burned with such acute awareness there was nothing the lake could do to extinguish her this time. Deep inside she heard her father, the Vizier, and the imagined voice of her mother, may God keep her, all scream, "Improper!" He doesn't care, she repeated to herself. He had no lustful motives. He wasn't capable of such thoughts.

Prince Eadmund gave a hearty approving laugh and said, "We're off!"

His strong arms and legs cut through the water without resistance. He swam so fast the breeze of his passing lifted the gauzy veil around Aminira's head.

She laughed suddenly, joyfully, unconsciously, at the memory of dolphins riding the wake of her ship on the sea voyage. They were faster than the ship, their grey bodies leaping out of the silver spray, there and gone. This must be what riding a dolphin was like.

"You have a pretty laugh. You should do it more often," Eadmund said and added his own mirth to hers.

The instant he called attention to her outburst, it ceased. Aminira smothered the laughter even though his comment had been kind. 'Give away nothing' had been drilled into her by father, uncle, and her comportment tutor. Advice which was designed to save her life in a palace full of vipcrous intrigue.

"Thank you," she mumbled, ashamed but determined to be polite, and deep inside, a little bit pleased.

The prince swam on, tirelessly pulling her through the water. At last he stopped.

"Here we are," he chuckled.

"What is it you wanted to show me?" Princess Aminira looked around. To the left was a tall sheer cliff which dropped straight into the water. She remembered riding beside it the night before on her mare. To the right, along a shimmery path of moonlight was an island so small it supported two tiny pine trees with no room to spare.

"There's a deep pool under this cliff. Deep enough to dive from the cliff without harm."

"Do you know this for certain?" Aminira looked up at the stone face and recalled her father throwing her overboard.

"Yes." Eadmund nodded. "I've swam to the bottom of the pool over and over." He gave an almost wistful sounding chuckle. "In summer children come here and dive off the cliff. I've always wanted to try it. What do you say?"

He turned to face her in the water and Aminira found herself hugging him, not just hanging on. She let go of him and tread water while backing up a little bit. The prince didn't seem to notice, his eager puppy expression never wavered.

"Come on, I can't do it on my own. Even if I got to the

top of the cliff I'd only drift down, if a breeze didn't take me first," he wheedled, still smiling.

Aminira looked up at the cliff. It seemed taller from water level than it had on horseback. She remembered the cliffs ranging about ten to fifteen feet high and no more.

She nodded. "All right."

The prince gave a delighted whoop and splashed water high into the air. "Race you to shore!" He dove into the water and in a second, he'd surfaced a few feet from the water's edge where he waited for her to catch up.

Aminira smiled. He knew he couldn't leave the water without her so he stood, knee-deep in the lake, grinning, waiting for her to win. Her feet touched the pebbled shore and she held out her hand. He took it and only then fully left the water.

"Come on, hurry." He pointed to the grassy slope which rose up, one face sheared off as if by a knife, falling straight into the water. His eager laughter launched him into the air. His hand tightened on hers but he only laughed harder.

"All right, come along," Aminira said and started up the slope, pulling Eadmund like a streamer behind her.

Once at the edge of the cliff she could see the drop wasn't too bad. Any higher and she may have refused the prince's request. How would this work? He would have weight again once they hit the water and he could land right on top of her. She thought for a moment running through various scenarios in her head, most of which involved the prince's suddenly heavy limbs knocking her in the head.

"What are you waiting for?" he giggled and poked her shoulder. "Let's go."

"All right. I think I have it figured out."

Aminira took the prince in her arms, as she had the

night before, like a groom carrying his bride. She backed up a few steps then ran toward the edge of the cliff.

Thrill and fear fluttered in her stomach. Eadmund screamed with laughter that almost sounded like panic. They hung for a fraction of a second in space, momentum pushing them away from the hilltop. Then gravity took hold and Aminira fell. She held tight to Eadmund as his arm tightened on her shoulders and his hysteric laughter echoed over the lake.

They plummeted together, her pulling the prince. A great spray of water went up as they hit, plunging deep, deeper, into the pool beneath the cliff.

The instant they hit the water Aminira let go of Eadmund. He would have been wrenched from her arms by the force of the water if she hadn't. Their limbs tangled and for a moment Aminira was afraid they'd drown. At last they separated and Aminira glimpsed silver moonlight seeping through the greenish water. She aimed for what she hoped was up and kicked.

Aminira broke the surface of the water and inhaled sweet, damp night air. She heard screaming and Aminira was afraid the prince had broken something when they'd hit the water.

She spun around, searching, and saw Eadmund a few feet away shrieking with laughter, unable to contain himself.

He saw her and swam near, gasping for air between bursts of laughter.

"How marvelous!" he cried, able to speak at last. "I've never felt that before! What a sensation! Fluttery and rippley and thrilling and fast! So fast! Again! I must go again." He swam toward shore, laughing all the way. His laughter infected Aminira so that by the time she joined him, she was laughing too.

CHAPTER 6

Princess Aminira looked at the lump in her bed and smiled, in too good a mood to even feel like she should feel affronted. Bea, her head newly shaven by the wagon master to keep the camels from getting her lice, lay curled in Aminira's bed, the lump of a pillow at her feet to make her look taller.

Despite being told there was no need, Bea had obviously taken it upon herself to 'stand in' for Aminira, impersonating the princess so Aminira wouldn't be missed in case anyone came looking. Not that anyone could mistake the malnourished girl for the much taller princess.

"Bea," Aminira whispered and shook the girl's shoulder.

Her eyes popped open, instant fear on her face. She relaxed when she saw the princess framed in the warm glow of the lamp. Aminira had come up the back stairs lighting her way with the amber lamp. She'd changed into her cotton nightdress.

"You're back." Bea grinned and scooted over, pulling

back the covers for Aminira.

The princess slid into bed and put the lamp on the nightstand.

"Did you see the prince?" Bea asked, rolling over to face Aminira.

"I did." Aminira smiled.

"Is he handsome?" Bea sighed.

"Very. He has light hair that looks almost white in the moonlight and a wonderful laugh."

"Are you going to marry him?" Bea asked.

Aminira laughed softly. "I met him two days ago. What sort of woman marries a man they only just met?"

"I guess," Bea said, her mouth turned down in disappointment. "But I think you'd make a great queen."

"Perhaps, one day," Aminira said. Despite her protests, on the ride back to the inn, Aminira had thought of nothing but Eadmund and wondered what kind of husband he would be. He would spend all his time in the lake. He would laugh at everything: trade negotiations, threats of war, politics, parties, all of it, no matter how dire or important. Even worse, what would happen if he passed on his curse to their children?

"Go to sleep," she told Bea as much as herself. "The future will sort itself out."

Bea's eyes slid shut and she let out a contented sigh. Aminira wished sleep would come as easily. Despite her words she wasn't sure the future would take care of itself, at least not without her intervention. She lay awake a long time listening to Bea's soft breaths, grateful for the girl's warm presence.

When Aminira was a child and couldn't sleep, her maid Meklit would get into bed with her and tell her stories until she fell asleep, just like other children's mothers would do. Meklit had been dismissed when the sultan found out. He wanted his daughter to grow up strong. Sentimentality was for the weak and the weak could not survive the Palace.

Her father would think Eadmund feeble. The sultan would surely disapprove. A cursed prince was in no way suitable for his daughter. Luckily, he was across the ocean and had no say. Eadmund might be cursed, but that didn't equal weakness. Besides, Aminira smiled as she pulled the blankets around herself, he made her laugh.

The next morning Aminira slept late and when she woke, Bea was gone. Up before the sun to go tend the camels.

Aminira forced herself through a set of practice sword strikes to get her blood flowing, then completed her prayers. Though late, she still offered her cants to God and hoped the Sun would bless her days in Lagobel. Then she rang for a maid. She wanted breakfast though it was closer to lunch, and a long, hot bath. The cold deep water of the lake, as well as the late nights, were getting to her. Her head felt stuffed with wool and her nose ran. Even so, she smiled as she recalled the prince's joy. They dove from the cliff over and over; each time Prince Eadmund thrilled as if it were the first. The sensation of falling, even that short plummet, was new and unfamiliar. He seemed to be making up for a lifetime of never having fallen. Aminira thought him lucky, for he had yet to fall and feel pain. She had fallen off horses, down stairs, tripped on paving stones, skinned knees and split her lip.

A sharp knock sounded on the door of her room, far

too sharp and loud for a maid, which meant it must be the Vizier. Aminira slipped into a long, embroidered dressing gown and wrapped a scarf around her head. No doubt when she rang for the maid it alerted Hamandir that she was up.

Princess Aminira opened the door of her room and said, "Good morning, Vizier." She gave him a rare big smile, big as the good feelings still lingering from last night's adventure with the prince.

The Vizier frowned. "May I come in, Your Highness?"

"Of course." She stepped aside. "I just rang the maid to have breakfast sent up."

"Yes, I know. It will be here in a moment," Hamandir said curtly.

Princess Aminira sat down on the sofa. Only after she was seated did he settle on the couch opposite her.

He produced a large envelope from his sleeve and said, "You have your wish. We are invited to the palace tomorrow night for whatever those barbarians consider a fête."

His sour mood and burning disapproval struck her funny. Aminira covered her mouth and laughed softly. Poor Hamandir had so far been appalled by everything on this journey. The first ball they attended had nearly shocked him to death. Couples of the opposite sex danced together, touching hands of all things. Aminira had been shocked as well but she hadn't expected customs to be the same as home, where dancing was performed in groups of the same sex.

"It will be the same as all the others," Aminira assured him. "Though perhaps more entertaining."

Hamandir's brow furrowed, a deep pit creasing the center of his forehead. "After that luncheon we can expect the worst. I beg you. I can have us resupplied and ready to go before the sun rises tomorrow. You can even bring that street urchin you found. The head groom says she has no family and agreed she will make a decent camel wrangler."

"Nonsense," Aminira said. "We shall accept the invitation and go to the party and we will have an excellent time."

He let out a longer, more suffering sigh than usual and said, "Very well. But I refuse to enjoy it."

Aminira laughed suddenly, the sound bubbled up, uncontainable as a sneeze. It burst out before she realized it was going to happen.

"Your Highness." The Vizier tried to sound cautionary but she thought she heard a touch of hurt.

"I'm sorry," she said. "If you don't wish to have fun I can't make you. But I encourage you to reconsider." Aminira had the urge to reach out and pat his hand but restrained herself. Princesses don't comfort underlings nor do respectable women touch men who are not their husbands. She was growing sick of rules that seemed to apply less and less the further from Qadarh she got.

"I would be happier knowing we were leaving. But," he added before she could say anything, "I will attend and smile for diplomacy's sake."

He stood and bowed. "And now, if you will excuse me, Your Highness, I must oversee preparations for the ball."

"Of course, Vizier. You may go," she said. She, too, had preparations to make. A gown to choose, jewelry, shoes, veil or turban or perhaps scarves draped with jewels. She would be formally introduced to Eadmund at last and wanted to look her best.

As soon as Vizier Hamandir left, Aminira started making

plans. She would ride out to see the prince tonight, talk to him about the ball. She wanted him to pretend they had not yet met. Knowing Eadmund he would think it a grand prank and have a long laugh. Aminira just didn't want to explain to the king and queen she had already befriended their son. And she really didn't want Vizier Hamandir to find out she'd met the prince in secret. He would quickly realize the true reason she insisted they stay in Lagobel.

The full moon had waned and seemed farther away, a bright but distant speck too far to illuminate the forest.

Aminira sat on the rock she'd slept on the first night she had met Prince Eadmund. Same as the previous night, she brought a glass lantern and extra candles to make up for the moon's waning light.

She listened to the soft splashes of fish, croaks of frogs, and chirr of insects. In a short time the lake had become dear to her. Perhaps because she had now spent so much time in its cold, gentle water. Someday she hoped to spend time on the water in daylight. Perhaps take a boat trip around the lake and take in the sights.

Aminira heard a loud splash and a wave of water doused her from behind. She gasped with cold shock and, without thinking, braced herself with her arms and kicked a leg out behind her. Her foot connected with something solid and she heard a wheeze. Spinning around she saw a pale flash sink into the water.

The prince. She'd just kicked him.

"Your Highness! Are you alright?" she called to the bubbles in the water. Aminira reached in, trying to find him. She couldn't have hurt him, could she? He was just playing another silly prank, sneaking up on her, but she should have told him not to. She'd been trained too well.

Her hands found nothing, just water and rock and slippery weeds. Aminira jumped into the water. Eadmund could be sinking to the rocky bottom of the lake.

She took a deep breath before diving under and heard him laughing. Hysteric peels of mirth echoed over the lake.

Aminira turned around and there he was, right behind her again, laughing his head off. She warmed all over, a combination of anger, relief, and embarrassment. Eadmund laughed harder when he saw the serious look on her face.

"Don't sneak up on me. I could have hurt you," Aminira said and climbed back onto her seat.

The prince giggle-snorted and said, "No, I'm fine. You got me though." He rubbed his chest. "That was certainly unexpected."

She let out a sigh. "I have been trained in combat from childhood. You must keep that in mind."

He laughed. "Yes, I will...Princess." Then he winked.

Aminira gaped at him. "How did you–the ball. Of course. But how do you know I'm a princess?"

Eadmund doubled over in the water and laughed as he sucked in some water. "I didn't for sure. Until now. But you seem a bit princessy. Good manners and well dressed. But not like the others I've met." He waved a hand in the air. "They were... I don't know... funny faced, but not amused." He stuck his nose in the air and turned it up making a sniffing noise. "Like that. They never smiled, not once! Can you believe it?" He dissolved in laughter. "Father keeps hoping one will marry me, but since I'm not wed, none must have said yes."

During their travels, she had met several princesses just as he described. Arrogant, Aminira would call them. But Eadmund didn't even have the words for an insult. And he hadn't insulted them really, just tried to describe them with accuracy.

"No prince back home would marry me either," Aminira said.

"I can't imagine why not," Eadmund said. "You are very fun."

"In Qadarh and its neighboring nations I was considered too manly. My father had no male heir and raised me as a boy." Aminira pursed her lips and waited to see what he made of this. Would he still like her after such a confession? Did he want someone more feminine? Many of the princes she'd met in Qadarh and even in these foreign parts, didn't want a wife who could best them in a sword duel.

Eadmund laughed, "You don't seem manly to me, but father says I'm a terrible judge of character since I like everyone."

"So, will you be at the ball?" She changed the subject, not wanting to find out more of what King Luberto hoped for in a wife for his son.

"Of course I will. Mother is insisting."

"Is that the only reason?" Aminira couldn't help asking, though she dreaded it might be. He seemed to love the lake more than a thousand glorious parties.

"Oh, no. Balls are quite fun. Music and food, and lots of people. I'll have to carry around some rocks all night so I can stay on the floor. Mother and father hate it when I spend the evening on the ceiling."

Aminira chuckled at the thought of the prince lying on the ceiling looking down on all the festivities.

Prince Eadmund swam closer to the rock Aminira occupied. He pulled himself out of the water and sat down on the edge; keeping his legs submerged just to be sure he wouldn't blow away. Aminira liked how normal it felt.

"So," Eadmund grinned, "what's this prank we are going to pull?"

"It's not very clever," Aminira said. She didn't want to get his hopes up. He looked a little too eager to trick his parents. "When we're introduced at the ball, pretend we've never seen each other before." It would raise too many questions Aminira didn't want to answer, like, 'Where did you meet and when?'

"Good idea." Eadmund snapped his fingers. "Parents are so nosy. I wonder if it is all parents or only kings and queens?" He giggled as he pondered the thought.

Aminira lowered her head and looked at the night-black water of the lake. She hadn't thought he'd be so sensible, or so clever as to understand her meaning. He wasn't stupid. He just wasn't serious. But it was easy to treat the lighthearted prince like a simpleton.

She let out a heavy sigh of disappointment because the Vizier wasn't there to do it for her. She was disappointed in herself for thinking so little of the prince.

"Can we go diving again? All day I dreamed about falling. It was so fun I hardly wanted to wake up. Then I remembered who had taken me diving and couldn't wait for nightfall." He laughed as if he'd told a grand joke, legs churning the water and sending ripples out over the lake.

Another compliment that made Aminira flush with heat from ear tips to toes. Of course it meant nothing, she reminded herself.

She smiled calmly and said, "Actually I was hoping you

could tell me where your aunt, the Princess Yisabelle, lives."

"Better yet, I can show you. Aunt Yisabelle has a castle on the north shore." Eadmund nodded. "She's a funny old thing. I don't think I've met her but twice." He giggled some more.

"Is that very far away?" Aminira asked.

"Come on. I'll show you." Prince Eadmund laughed and grabbed her hand. He pulled her into the water and wrapped her arm around his neck. "Hang on. I'm going to swim as fast as I can."

She held on. In only a minute the rock was left behind, the lantern a distant twinkle like a star, then that was lost as well.

As he swam, he chatted between fits of laughter. He told Aminira about another accident from his childhood.

Once, when he was a little boy, he'd caught a frog. He wanted to show the frog to his father who had just entered the gardens with a full retinue on account of some visiting dignitary. With a sack of rocks to keep him anchored in one hand and an amphibian in the other, Eadmund launched himself at his father, making a huge slow leap over the hedgerows. Unfortunately the young prince miscalculated and instead of presenting the frog to his father, he smacked the visiting dignitary in the face with the unfortunate creature.

Eadmund laughed so ferociously telling her the story, they were forced to tread water until he could get his breath back. Aminira was a little afraid he'd never recover. Even so, she couldn't help laughing at the story herself.

They reached the north side of the lake quicker than Aminira would have thought. The lake seemed endless from the south, the view of its far shores obscured by hills and islands.

Eadmund slowed and Aminira let go of his neck and swam beside him. They approached a narrow wedge shaped castle that jutted over the water, taking advantage of the stony shore for its foundations. The tallest tower looked as if it rose from the water, arrow straight, the pointed roof stabbed at the sky.

Floating blue-green lights danced along the outer walls. Witch lights. The castle windows, what few were lit, shared the watery hues. Aminira pursed her lips. She shivered as the cold crept through her skin and froze her bones. The frigid water seemed colder here than it had elsewhere.

"Aunt Yisabelle's castle," Eadmund said and chuckled softly. Even his voice was low, as if this place cowed his buoyant spirits.

"She must have great power," Aminira whispered, instinctively afraid to raise her voice. Or was it something else? A spell to frighten visitors? Witches often used such tricks to seem more powerful than they were.

Eadmund giggled and Aminira thought it sounded nervous. "If she has so much power she ought to smile more. I would if I could do magic. It must be great fun."

"We should go." Her whisper sounded desperate and frightened. Aminira cleared her throat and said, "I need to rest before the ball. There is a lot to prepare for tomorrow."

He nodded and spun in the water. "I'll show you how fast I can really swim."

"You've been holding back?"

"Maybe a little." He grinned over his shoulder.

Aminira put her arms around him, glad to leave the witch's castle behind, and glad Eadmund was inclined to leave quickly. She would have been ashamed of running away if she hadn't remembered her lessons on military strategy. She could hear her father saying, 'There is no shame in retreat. The only shame is not coming back stronger.'

CHAPTER 7

Lagobel's palace, decorated in silk banners and glowing paper lanterns, welcomed Aminira to the ball. She stepped out of the carriage, pulling the skirts of her gown after her.

Bea had tried to talk her into riding a camel to the ball but Aminira flatly refused. She wasn't about to risk a camel spitting on her and ruining her dress, which was exactly the sort of thing a camel would do, possibly on purpose. The sly beasts seemed to know exactly what not to do and then did it.

Her silk dress rustled as the Vizier himself held the carriage door for her. Ignoring all the Vizier's sighs and frowns, she had worn the northern style gown, with a few additions for her own comfort, not to appease the Vizier's disapproval.

The gown was blue-grey silk embroidered with silver and crystal. The bodice was too low cut for comfort and the undergarments required to wear the dress pushed her breasts up, no doubt the reason the bodice dipped so low. Aminira solved the problem by wearing a long sleeved cotton blouse beneath the dress and an extra long blue veil that covered not only her head but shoulders and chest as well. Crowning the veil was a small silver and moonstone tiara. The Vizier refused to go so far and say he liked the ensemble but on the ride to the palace she had seen him scrutinize the outfit for faults in modesty, and finding none, he was forced to complain about the possible food, King Luberto's atrocious manners, and the weather instead.

Liveried footmen lined the steps leading up to the castle, identical and stiff as tin soldiers. One of them on the highest stair broke ranks, bowed low, and said, "Please follow me, Your Highness."

The footman marched through the great hall, keeping far enough ahead to guide them unobtrusively. When they reached the ballroom the footman said to an even fancier servant, "Her Royal Highness, Princess Aminira Elamalesha and guest."

The Vizier bristled at the label 'guest' and before the fancy servant could announce to the room their names, he said, "I'm Lord High Vizier Wahid Hamandir. And you better get it right."

Princess Aminira looked at him, eyebrow raised. 'Lord High' was a new addition to his title. The Vizier shrugged.

With a gulp, the servant announced them to the room. His voice echoed off the high ceiling of the ballroom which was cleverly painted to look like a blue sky with delicate clouds floating overhead.

To the left was a receiving line where the king, queen, and prince stood greeting guests. The fancy servant turned and bowed, pointing the Princess and the self-anointed

Lord High Vizier toward their hosts.

Princess Aminira felt the eyes of the Lagobel nobles on her. They watched the foreign princess with curiosity, judging her clothes, bearing, and looks. She had always avoided state occasions even back home where they didn't wear the guise of parties. But she looked around the room with her best semi-aloof smile, nodding to those who smiled back.

"Welcome." King Luberto threw his arms out as Aminira approached. For a moment, she was afraid he would hug her. His arms dropped to his sides and he looked her over. "No dagger tonight? You should have brought it."

"I'm sure I'll have no need," she replied as she curtsied. He had a good eye. The bejeweled scabbard she'd worn to lunch looked purely ornamental but the dagger was useful in a pinch. One thing the north lands shared with her home, virtually no one at court went unarmed.

King Luberto grunted, unconvinced. "Let me introduce my son."

Aminira heard the reluctance in King Luberto's voice. Shame and embarrassment mixed with resignation. She felt bad for Eadmund and annoyed with King Luberto for the first time. He must be disappointed with his son, but it wasn't Eadmund's fault he was cursed.

Queen Gwinden squared her shoulders and glared at her husband. "My son, Prince Eadmund." She pulled him forward.

Princess Aminira curtsied to him. Grinning, he bowed, gave her a wink, and burst out laughing. Aminira froze, rigid with horror. Everyone must know they knew each other. He'd given away the entire ruse and now she'd have to explain their acquaintance to everyone.

She glanced at the king and queen. King Luberto looked at the ceiling, a vein standing out on his forehead she swore hadn't been there a second ago. Queen Gwinden pinched her son's arm while she stared very hard at some paint on the far wall of the ballroom.

"Eadmund, introduce yourself properly," Queen Gwinden said.

Prince Eadmund bowed again, bobbing slightly in the air. He held two round stones, one in each hand and there were two more tied to his ankles, but he still drifted like a boat moored to a pier. "A pleasure to meet you, Princess Aminira. You grace us with your presence." He managed to get the words out with little more than a giggle at the beginning but he broke down once his speech was over. His braying laugh echoed around the room, drowning out the musicians for a second.

"The pleasure is mine, Prince Eadmund," she curtsied deeply.

"Please go and enjoy the ball," King Luberto said, face red under his pale beard.

"Thank you, Your Majesty." Aminira nodded and left the receiving line. Vizier Hamandir bowed as he swept along behind her.

"What an odd curse," the Vizier said once they were far from the king and queen.

"Indeed," Aminira agreed blandly.

The Vizier studied her closely, dark eyes narrowed and gauging. "Did the Prince wink at you?"

Aminira silently cursed Hamandir's powers of observation. Of course he was trained to, just as she was. Be silent and watchful.

"I don't know what you're talking about, Lord High

Vizier," she said pointedly, distracting him by turning the conversation back to his earlier 'self-promotion'.

He reddened and covered his discomfort with a cough. "They should introduce me by title, not as a guest," he grumbled.

"Of course. And now you have the opportunity to enlighten them." She pointed out a group of nobles dressed in fine silks, among them several pretty ladies who watched the princess and the Vizier with open curiosity.

"And what will you do?" he asked even as he stroked his beard, making sure it was smooth.

"I am going to eat dinner and mingle with Lagobel's high society." The same thing she had done in every kingdom at every ball thrown in her honor. Though in truth, she was biding her time until Prince Eadmund was done with the receiving line.

An hour later, Aminira had met a dozen or so Dukes, Duchesses, a couple of Earls, Counts and Countesses, a very chatty Lord and Lady, and a presumptuous Baron who had traveled to the Princess's part of the world and proceeded to tell her all about her homeland as though she had not been born and raised there.

She kept on eye on the receiving line and saw the king and queen break and head out into the crowd. The prince drifted away, too, held down by the smooth stones around his ankles and the ones held in his hand. He walked in short leaps that bounced him across the room.

He paused to talk to people along the way, mostly nobles, but she saw him stop a few servants as they made their rounds with trays of food and drinks. The prince would say something then laugh, and for a moment, the sound echoed around the room, bouncing off the high ceiling.

Inevitably the servant broke decorum and laughed along with the Prince, smiling fondly at him.

How much of his good nature was his own and how much part of the curse? Aminira's heart squeezed tight at the thought that Eadmund's open and funny personality was just a byproduct of the curse. He was joyful because he didn't know any better. He treated everyone equally because he had not the gravity and arrogance to do otherwise. If she broke the curse, would he turn into another spoiled, imperious prince growing fat off the hard work of the peasants? Or perhaps breaking the curse would only temper his mirth with kindness and empathy.

She kept him in the corner of her eye as he hop-skipped about the room talking to everyone. Even the grimmest faced noble of the court couldn't help a smile when Eadmund stopped and chatted with them.

Eventually, the Prince made his way to Aminira's group and interrupted their frivolous discussion with a polite bow. Or at least close approximation of a bow. He tipped forward and only the rounded stones tied to his boots kept him from pitching into a spin.

"Your Highness." Aminira dipped her knees. She fought the urge to push him upright.

He straightened up, laughter spilling out. "Good evening, Your Highness, are you enjoying the ball?"

"Very much," she said.

"You haven't danced yet," he said and giggled.

Aminira was surprised he'd noticed. Maybe he wasn't as oblivious as she thought. "No, Your Highness, I have not."

"Good. That means I'm first." He tried a sweeping bow but his body angled backward.

"Would you care to dance, Princess Aminira?"

"I would, thank you," she said. "Though I hope you don't mind if I'm not terribly good."

Prince Eadmund doubled over with uproarious laughter and Aminira's smile strained almost to breaking. She glanced around the ballroom but no one took any heed of the Prince's barrage. She received a few pitying glances from the noble ladies and a disapproving glare from the Vizier.

The Prince tilted in the air as he said, "I'm a terrible dancer, and you'll have to lead!" He set the rocks he held down on a table next to the dance floor and offered her his hand.

She held onto it, keeping him from bouncing too high. He was extra buoyant with only the stones tied to his shoes.

As they stepped onto the dance floor, other couples made way, giving them room. Aminira thought it was out of respect for a royal couple, but she soon saw a few tart looks directed at the prince from young nobles and a few even deserted the floor entirely.

Her heart sank. Perhaps she shouldn't have said yes so quickly. They moved to the center of the floor and resigned Aminira, steeled herself to become a spectacle. Laugh as they might, Aminira would not be cowed by the foreign nobles. She was not over fond of being the center of attention, but she certainly knew how to hold her own with confidence. She raised her chin and squared her shoulder.

The music started. A lively tune, and Aminira knew the steps accompanying it. Step forward, back, half turn left, and clap, half turn right and clap, then come together for a circle, part, come together, circle again and repeat until the music ends.

Aminira took the first step toward Prince Eadmund and

he tried to take a step toward her but he blew forward and crashed into her. She caught him in her arms and set him up right again. He laughed so hard he skipped the half turn and gave a weak clap along with the other dancers. He managed the second half turn but had a hard time getting back around.

Aminira grabbed the Prince's hands as they came together for the circle. He was almost hysterical with laughter.

He looked at her as she tried to focus on the dance steps and imitated her frown. "If you keep making that face I'll never stop laughing."

"You never stop laughing anyway," Aminira snapped. She regretted the words as they left her mouth. She was frustrated with the dance, just as he had promised, he was terrible. But it wasn't Eadmund's fault.

Aminira saw the twinkle in his eyes. His mocking frown fell away and he smiled, dazzlingly, genuine. She felt a flutter tickle her chest and her frown disappeared.

She laughed suddenly and loudly.

"See?" he said. "It's dancing, it's supposed to be fun."

Laughter still bubbling from some unknown well inside her, Aminira took Eadmund's hand in hers and put an arm around his waist. He said she'd have to lead after all...

He put a steadying hand on her shoulder and she pulled the Prince across the polished stone floor. She whirled him around following no dance she knew, making one up a she went along. His feet barely touched the ground as they turned and hopped, her laughter joining his, their voices adding their own notes and rhythm to the jaunty tune the musicians played.

The other dancers fell away, retreating from their whirling unpredictable path until Aminira and Eadmund had the floor to themselves.

"Spin me around," Eadmund said. Aminira took his hands and spun, the prince's feet left the ground and he screamed with delight like a little boy. She put him down and picked him up at the waist, twirling again.

His face was flushed under his sun browned skin. His pale hair, bleached almost white by hours spent in the sun, whipped in the air.

"How high can you throw me?" He grinned, eyes challenging her.

"Let us see." She smiled back. She swung her arms, throwing him into the air. Scattered applause broke out as Prince Eadmund soared high, higher, slowing just before he touched the hanging crystals of a chandelier.

He fell down, slowly but steadily, pulled by the stones ties on his boots.

Aminira reached up and caught Eadmund in her arms just as the music stopped.

Wild applause filled the ballroom and Aminira's already warm face ignited with joy. She turned, smiling at the crowd even as she set Eadmund on his feet. He bowed to the clapping nobles, one arm still around her shoulders to keep from floating off.

Vizier Hamandir scowled at her, disapproval radiating from his entire being. There would be no distracting him now.

Beyond the Vizier, the king and queen stood beaming at her. She studied them. Indeed, they looked at her, not their son. Queen Gwinden clapped politely a few times, her eyes measuring Aminira carefully. King Luberto leaned over and whispered something to his wife. Her eyebrows quirked, one rising toward the pale line of her hair.

What did that look signify? Had she been too enthusiastic? Maybe she was the laughing stock she had feared earlier. One could never go wrong with formality. Her cool smile returned. "Thank you for the dance." She curtsied to Prince Eadmund.

"I've never had so much fun at a ball," Eadmund said. "And I never get to dance like that. Most people don't like to dance with me."

A hollow trumpet blast announced a late comer to the ball. The sound cut off Aminira's reply, the single long echoing note cut down all other sounds leaving an eerie silence in its wake.

Aminira turned to the entry and saw an old woman in a finely cut black gown trimmed with delicate lace. Her hair was white and twisted into thick braids held by a gold tiara. Wrinkles carved into the skin around her eyes and mouth, indeed only tiny glittering beads could be seen of her eyes, and her face was set in glaring disapproval.

"Aunt Yisabelle," Prince Eadmund whispered. He still grinned, but it seemed strained, as though he smiled against his will.

King Luberto's sister smiled, somehow her mouth stayed down-turned but it was a smile. She glided down the steps and the court curtsied and bowed and parted before her.

The energy drained from the room and Aminira glanced up at the chandelier above. The candles seemed to grow dim but she couldn't be sure.

Vizier Hamandir materialized at her side. He pulled a dagger from his sleeve and slipped it into Aminira's hand. She wasn't sure what good the dagger would do against a witch but she felt better for having it and silently praised the Vizier's foresight in bringing it.

Yisabelle's frown-smile deepened as she approached Eadmund, sharpening the lines around her mouth. His grin stayed fixed, a frozen rictus. He giggled but it sounded nervous.

Heart thudding with a mix of fear and disbelief, Aminira stepped forward. She put herself between Yisabelle and Eadmund. She knew she was supposed to be pretending she had just met him, and of course she had known him only days, but she couldn't leave him unprotected to the whims of the woman who had cursed him. The witch's eyes flashed from blue to dark maroon. Aminira blinked, unsure she had really seen Yisabelle's eyes change color, though nothing was impossible when dealing with a witch.

Before Yisabelle could reach Prince Eadmund and Aminira, King Luberto shoved his way through the cowering nobles, pushing aside those who would not or could not move.

"Yisabelle," he bellowed, voice cracking through the deadened atmosphere. "What are you doing here?" Luberto stopped Yisabelle before she could reach his son.

"I was invited," Yisabelle said, her eyes glittered pinkish-red. She stared only at Prince Eadmund, ignoring Luberto, ignoring the crowd huddled on the edges of the ballroom.

"Well, yes," Luberto said, "but you never come."

"I decided it was time to visit. Been ages, hasn't it? When was the last time I came to court?" Yisabelle's smile showed small and too numerous teeth, like a snarl. "Ah, yes. My dear nephew's naming day."

At that, King Luberto turned purple with rage. He was a head shorter than his sister but he seemed to swell, puffing up like a hooded cobra. "How dare you."

"How dare I what? It almost sounds like you have

something to accuse me of, dear brother."

The king's mouth chewed on unspoken words. Aminira suspected he feared what the witch might do if dragged into the open. Did she have the power to threaten the entire kingdom? Or would she finish off her nephew?

"Come, dear boy, let me see how you've grown." Yisabelle held out an ivory hand, thick and ropy blue veins wormed beneath her skin.

Prince Eadmund gave a nervous giggle again, but didn't move. Aminira stepped forward instead, dagger tucked in her sleeve. She bowed to the Princess and said, "Good evening, Your Highness. Please allow me to introduce myself. I am Princess Aminira Elamalesha from Qadarh."

At last, Yisabelle's eyes left Prince Eadmund. Her spiteful green gaze raked over Princess Aminira. Impossibly, the witch princess showed more teeth and nodded to Aminira with the barest passing glance that etiquette would allow. "Princess, I know you've barely been here a week, but you've gotten to see some of our fair kingdom. Yes? The lake perhaps?"

The blood drained from Aminira's face. Guilt blossomed in her heart. Had she provoked Yisabelle when she'd asked Eadmund to show her the witch's castle? But how? And why had Yisabelle come now? Aminira didn't know but it couldn't be a coincidence that Yisabelle had shown up after all these years. Almighty Providence must be at work. First meeting the prince alone in the woods, and now the witch who cursed him.

Aminira squared her shoulders and met the witch's gaze. "I have seen only a little of Lagobel, Your Highness. I've been to the palace twice, toured the city a bit, and been to the lake. Lagobel is a lovely kingdom, as you say." Her head spun but her voice was firm. No regular blade could cut down magic, but Aminira had brought such means with her. If only they weren't packed away in her luggage. Djinn scorch her alive, why had she not unpacked the protective amulet at least? She had been too addled with thoughts of her prince. Aminira hid her clenched fist in the folds of her gown. Her palm itched to pull the dagger.

"The lake is the jewel in Lagobel's crown. My nephew takes its pleasures constantly, don't you, dear boy?"

He giggled again. "Yes. Except when the lake is iced over in winter."

"Why, I would venture to say you love the lake, don't you, my boy." Yisabelle stared at Aminira, flat eyes granite hard, the color of dried blood.

The witch was working her way up to something. Aminira felt the jaws closing around her, not knowing the shape or goal of the beast coming from her.

"Lake water must run in your veins for you to love it so," Yisabelle said, voice a purring whisper.

Eadmund laughed louder this time, his trepidation, if it had been there at all, soothed by the small talk. "I do love the water. I think it wonderful luck to have a lake right next to me."

"That's enough, Yisabelle," Luberto said. "You've talked to the boy."

Aminira's hand tightened on the dagger hilt. She had the urge to plunge it into the witch's heart though there was no logical reason. It was a feeling. Sweat broke over her with the effort to restrain herself. But why? The witch made no threat and Aminira couldn't just murder a foreign princess.

"Yes, enough chatting, Auntie Yisabelle." Eadmund chuckled. "Aren't you going to get some food or drink?

Or dance?" His open smile showed no fear. He turned the conversation because he didn't notice anything amiss

"Indeed, Yisabelle, we put out a very good spread, if I do say so myself," King Luberto said, not so much eager as relieved by the change of topic. He gestured to the tables laid out with plates of food.

Yisabelle turned slowly, eyes still on Aminira as she stepped away. She wasn't sure what she'd done to draw the witch's attention but Aminira repressed a shiver until Yisabelle was no longer looking. She wouldn't give the witch the satisfaction.

"Would you care for another dance?" Prince Eadmund asked.

Vizier Hamandir made a noise of disapproval. He wouldn't say so out loud but Aminira could tell he was dying to grab her, put her in a carriage, and drive until they were three kingdoms away from Lagobel and its witch.

"One more dance." Aminira held up her finger, "and a bit more sedate this time, I think. Then, perhaps we should go." Aminira wished to stay but that didn't seem wise. If they appeared to be too close, perhaps the witch would strike. Maybe she would anyway.

Aminira let Prince Eadmund lead her to the dance floor once more as the silent musicians resumed. She was careful to stick to the formal steps of the dance and watched as Luberto and Queen Gwinden tried to keep Yisabelle's attention on anything but their son.

She curtsied as the musicians finished the last few flourishes of the dance.

"Will I see you tonight?" Prince Eadmund nodded toward the ballroom's open balcony which overlooked the lake.

"I am afraid this is all the time we have tonight," Aminira replied.

"Oh?" He blinked. There was a moment of hesitation before he smiled and said, "Very well." He laughed briefly and picked up the smooth stones he'd left on the table. "I'll see you soon."

Instant, near painful regret cut into her. The prince seemed sorry that she'd sent him away. Maybe even hurt? Or was she imagining it? Aminira wanted to call him back, see if she could pry open his single and singular joy, to find out if something else was underneath.

Vizier Hamandir glided up behind her the moment Prince Eadmund was out of earshot.

"We should go, Your Highness." He tugged the fabric of her sleeve in his desperation, careful not to actually lay a hand upon her. "Please."

"Yes." Aminira nodded with slow agreement. She looked again at Yisabelle, who chose that second to look up, their eyes met across the room and this time Aminira shivered involuntarily. The witch's smile-frown deepened at the corners.

CHAPTER 8

For the next three nights Aminira stayed away from Prince Eadmund. She tossed and turned in her bed at the inn, aching to visit him but fearing to bring the witch's wrath down on Eadmund. Aminira cursed the timing of the witch's arrival. She must be planning something the question was, did Aminira's arrival have something to do with it? Did the witch want to ruin Eadmund's joy? But how could she, since the prince enjoyed everything equally? Maybe it was the king she wanted to punish further. Whatever feud lay between the king and his sister, Aminira knew she was missing enough pieces that she couldn't yet complete the picture.

She told Vizier Hamandir to quietly supply the caravan while Aminira played the part of visiting princess, attending feasts and accepting the hospitality of the nobility.

Who would the witch strike at? Would she demand Aminira leave the Kingdom? A possibility she was preparing for though not one she looked forward to. Pain, sometimes in her chest and sometimes in her stomach, haunted her. Every thought of leaving Lagobel and the prince made it worse. She told herself not to be stupid. Prince Eadmund wouldn't even miss her. He would laugh the same whether she stayed or went. He did not, could not, love or care for her.

Several times a day she almost talked herself into announcing they were to leave. The caravan could get underway in mere hours. Each time the orders were on her lips, ready to give to Vizier Hamandir, she held back.

Aminira told herself that if the witch's attentions were her fault, she should stay and deal with whatever happened next. She had a duty to do so, even as her heart whispered it was not duty alone that kept her in Lagobel.

Her fingers trailed in the brown black water, sending out ripples that were swallowed by the pleasure boat's wake. A dozen of the canopied craft leisurely skimmed the surface of the lake each one laden with rugs, pillows, food, a servant at the oars, and the noblemen and women of the court who King Luberto favored when he sent the invitations.

Princess Aminira had been invited on King Luberto's own ornate craft and the short robust King rowed vigorously himself. The servants went too slow he complained, and he'd shoved the man aside and ordered him to stay on the dock.

Luberto rowed with the same restless angry energy he did most things, a determined scowl on his face.

When he had pulled far ahead of the other boats, Luberto stopped rowing and they drifted on the glassy surface of the water. The King wiped his brow with a white handkerchief and cleared his throat.

"Nice day, this," Luberto said.

"Yes, Your Majesty," Aminira agreed, surprised by his attempt at small talk. He'd seemed so purposeful as he rowed, she expected more. Perhaps Yisabelle had demanded Aminira be thrown out of the country and he wanted to tell her in private.

"Princess Aminira, I have something I want to ask you and it's not easy."

Her heart sank into the black depths of the water. Her guess was correct.

"Your Majesty, I—"

"I'm not good at speeches." Luberto held up a hand and Aminira fell silent. "It will take a minute for me to work around to my point and I'd appreciate you just listen and not interrupt." He wiped his face again, growing, if anything, redder and sweatier than his exertions had already made him.

Aminira nodded solemnly. Being quiet and listening were two skills she excelled in.

King Luberto began, "I know my son is a fool, laughing off everything and everyone. He's not much of a catch, being cursed and all. Goodness knows we tried. His original arranged marriage fell apart and no one wants him. I don't blame them. He's laughed in the face of every princess we've managed to drag in. And I've got no other heirs. Yisabelle has no children any—" he cut himself off and ran a hand through his beard. "She has no heirs either…

"But Lagobel is a good kingdom. Prosperous, fine land, farming, pasture, timber…We're small, but we have a big heart, I like to say. I know it's not what you're used to though. Anyway, I can't leave Lagobel to my idiot son. Can you imagine? He'd laugh at every crisis, every diplomat, and every natural disaster. Lagobel would be invaded at the first opportunity," Luberto paused, staring out over the lake, face carved by troubles. He sighed, then looked at Aminira. "You, on the other hand, seem like a sensible girl. You seem to know how to use that sword you wear and I sent messengers to the last few Kingdoms you visited. Got the messenger pigeons back yesterday. Seems you're in the market for a husband. Gwinden and I saw you dance with Eadmund at the ball. Didn't look like you hated it." Luberto waggled his eyebrows at Aminira.

She sat, confused by the King's long speech. He wasn't trying to get rid of her, he sounded more like a rug merchant trying to sell an ill-woven carpet. 'It's not very pretty, but with the proper furniture it could look good in your house.'

King Luberto scowled at her intently and waited for her to say something. Aminira wasn't sure what question had been asked.

Finally Luberto growled and snapped, "Well? Will you marry my fool son or not? The Kingdom will be yours, the whole country. He might rule in name but you'd be making all the decisions. And the gods know you'll make better ones than Eadmund ever could. Lagobel would effectively be yours."

Stunned, Aminira sat in silence, mind not quite ready to respond. Her heart however, replied with a quickened joyful beat that seemed to pound out a fervent, yes. She tried to quell the rebellious organ and think things through.

King Luberto was, in his mind, proposing a political arrangement. He was king, and beyond seeing to his son's happiness, the future of a nation rested on his head.

The proposal made perfect, logical sense. She was indeed looking for a tolerable husband, someone to rule with, not be subject too. Her uncle had it right. She did want to rule. She just didn't want to shed blood to do so.

"We have only just met," Aminira said at last. It was the last barrier her mind kept putting up. What sort of woman marries a man she barely knows? Yet, that would have been her exact plight had one of the princes back home said yes to her father. She had never thought to marry for love. Or had she? At home she would have quietly done her duty as ordered by the Sultan. But she was on her own as never before. The choice was entirely hers. What was she still afraid of?

"He is as you see," Luberto said. "Not much depth to the boy I'm afraid. He's not learned or smart, and has one emotion. But I see what you mean. Please, stay and get to know Eadmund."

The King looked out over the lake. Brightening, he said, "Look there. Speak of the gods and expect a portend."

Prince Eadmund swam among the boats, going from one to another, not staying even as voices called him back.

Luberto cupped a beefy hand around his mouth and hollered, "Hoy! Over here."

Hearing his father's voice, Eadmund left off the boat he was swimming toward and made straight for the source.

With unnatural speed he bobbed to the surface of the water near the king's boat and pulled himself halfway from the water. The prince's face contorted as if some other emotion was trying to push through his wide grin. He let out a high pitched simpering giggle that didn't sound right to Aminira.

"Excellent timing, my boy," Luberto said.

"Father," Eadmund giggled again but it sounded pained and his brows wriggled, as if trying to knot but unable to do so.

"What is it?" Luberto asked.

Aminira wasn't sure but it seemed even the blustery King noticed something wrong with his son. She sat straighter on the cushioned seat of the boat, anxious to catch the prince's words.

"The lake. It's...lower."

"It's summer, of course the lake is lower."

"No," Prince Eadmund said, but he sounded unsure. "Maybe."

"Perhaps it is just lower than most years," Aminira said, trying to reassure him.

The prince seemed to notice her for the first time and he winced even as he smiled at her. "Ah, Princess Aminira. I haven't seen you since the ball. Have you been busy?"

Was that reproach? Had he actually missed her? Aminira said, "Yes. I have been. I'm sorry."

"Maybe I'll see you later?" His head twitched in what she thought was the direction of the beach. Their beach.

"Yes, certainly," she said. Unless she guessed wrong, Aminira thought, he was trying to set up a meeting at night like their first few. Witch or no, she would meet him. Eadmund seemed upset, if that were even possible. There was a crack in his perfect happiness and she needed to find out what was wrong.

He laughed at her reply, sounding closer to normal. "Later then. I'm going to swim the lake, see if something could account for the lowering. Perhaps one of the rivers is blocked"

The prince kicked away and was gone with a splash.

★★★

Prince Eadmund stood in waist high water waiting for Aminira. He laughed, loud and high pitched, like a night bird crying out over the lonely water He waved and took two steps toward shore. He wrung his hands and his smile was more grimace than happy-to-see-her.

"What's wrong?" Aminira called out as she slid off her horse.

"The water is lower, I'm sure," he said and stepped closer to the beach until the lake sloshed around his knees.

Aminira met him in the water. The Prince still smiled, still let out fitful giggles, but he seemed wan. In the lantern light, dark smudges beneath his eyes showed through his tan skin and his shoulders hunched.

"Did you find a cause?" Aminira asked. Before she could stop herself, she reached out and put a hand on his bare shoulder. Prince Eadmund seemed so upset, despite his smiles, that kindness was called for.

He didn't flinch from her touch but he didn't calm down either. "The rivers… seem less somehow."

"I'm sure there is a mistake. Perhaps the lake is just lower than it has been since you began swimming."

"No, no," he shook his head and let out a high pitched hopeless giggle. "Come, I'll show you." He took her hand and pulled her deeper into the water.

As before, Aminira put her arms around his shoulders and he swam them out to the deep waters of the lake.

A rocky grouping of stones, too small to make an island or even sprout a single plant, broke the cool black surface of the water. The Prince swam up to the rocks and tread water. Aminira let go of him so she could get a better view of whatever it was he'd taken her to see.

"There." Prince Eadmund pointed to a rock. "You see?"

Aminira squinted into the night, with only starlight to go by she was nearly blind. When she looked with the edge of her vision she saw a white line just above the water.

"The water line?" she asked.

"Exactly." The Prince laughed. "The white marks are waterlines, the lowest are winter, the highest summers. The lake is just below the lowest winter. It wasn't like that a few days ago. The lake is lowering."

Aminira turned her head, trying to see better, but the lines were too faint for her to trace the history of the waters. She wasn't sure he was right. How could so much water disappear? She had no real experience of lakes, not like Lagobel's. No oasis in her country boasted as much water as the lake held. She didn't know if Prince Eadmund was worried over nothing or if something else was at play.

"You say this water level is unusual and new?"

"Yes. I noticed it today when I got in the lake. I could feel it, like wearing woolen hose, sort of scratchy," he chuckled.

She put her hand on the rock, feeling for the scale mineral deposits indicating the waterline. She could barely feel a roughening of the stone.

"Perhaps we could row out here tomorrow when the sun is up. I could see more then," she suggested.

"Yes, yes, that's a good idea." Eadmund nodded. "We can meet at the Royal pier in the palace gardens at noon. I'll have the servants pack a lunch for you."

A wistful smile tugged the corners of her mouth. What he suggested sounded like a romantic outing and she wished that it were so.

"Has your father spoken to you recently about anything

important?" Aminira asked. Her face grew hot and despite the cool water encasing her, she began to sweat.

The Prince cocked his head. "He told me the lake is my imagination." He laughed. "Silly father. He's wrong about that."

King Luberto had not told his son about the proposed marriage. Aminira wasn't sure what she felt. Relief, disappointment, and the vague wish that Eadmund himself would come to the conclusion of marriage on his own without the king's prompting.

"Prince Eadmund." Aminira dug into her reserve of courage and put her hand on his where it pressed against the rock. "Do you like me?"

He laughed the realest and warmest laugh of the night. "Of course, I like you, you're fun."

"No more than that?"

"Well, you're pretty, and you danced with me and went swimming and we jumped off the cliff which was amazing," Prince Eadmund said, adding a fond chuckle.

What was she expecting? More to the point, a kingdom had been handed to her, the chance to rule on her own terms, not be ruled by a husband. Why did she hesitate? Aminira wasn't sure. She wanted him to love her but knew it wasn't possible.

"Do you like me more than the lake?" Aminira asked.

Eadmund blinked at the question, his smile turned to a grin and he gazed up at the stars as he said, "That's like asking if I like my heart or my blood more."

Heat tinged her cheeks. That was probably as close to a declaration of love the Prince could come to. After all, without a heart, or without blood, he would die.

"Does that mean you can't live without me?" Aminira

asked, trying to sound teasing but she was sincere. Fearing the answer, she stared at the cluster of rocks and wished she was made of the same cold stone.

"Live?" the Prince chuckled softly. "Perhaps. Though life would be much duller. You are the funnest princess I have ever met."

Aminira couldn't help the laughter that spilled out of her. "No one has ever called me fun before, not even as a child," she said. "At home I was silent and lifeless. You would never have recognized me."

"Then you must never leave," the Prince declared, voice bubbling over with hilarity. "You must stay here and have fun with me."

"Do you mean that?" Her stomach fluttered, happy and anxious, and she knew even if he meant it, he didn't mean it how she wanted him to.

"Of course," he grinned. "I must convince someone to fly me as a kite."

"That is still a terrible idea." She chuckled and shook her head.

Eadmund smiled and sighed. "Let's go back. I'm getting tired, I think."

"Tired?" Aminira's good humor dissipated and blew away like desert sand. "Are you all right? Are you ill?" She had been amazed by his energy since she had met the prince. To say he was tired seemed so out of character. Perhaps he was right about the lake. Or maybe his aunt was behind the symptom.

He shook his head. "I feel..." His smile tightened with thought. "I don't know. But tired is close."

"Of course we can go back," she agreed. "If you like, I can take you to the Palace on my horse."

"No. I can swim back," he said.

"Are you sure? What if you fall asleep and drown?"

"What a funny idea," he giggled. "No, I'll be fine. I just need some rest."

Aminira chewed her lip. She wished she could see the Prince's face well enough to look for physical signs of illness. But what did she know? She knew more about spotting illness in hawks than in humans.

"Come on." He pushed away from the rocks. She put her arms around him so he could take her back to shore.

CHAPTER 9

Princess Aminira stood on the royal dock. She wore an ivory turban like the first time she had met the prince. This time a sapphire brooch with a cascade of diamonds was pinned to the silk.

She had made up her mind. She would marry the Prince. She would tell King Luberto and her own dear Vizier, who paced a few feet away, after her outing with the Prince. For Luberto, it would be no great surprise. Hopefully he had informed Queen Gwinden about the proposal. The Vizier would not be pleased. Aminira would have to have a long talk with him.

A mischievous smile curled her lips. Poor Vizier Hamandir, he was in for an unpleasant surprise. Aminira was a little sorry now she had gotten his hopes up resupplying the caravan. Now that her decision was made, Princess Aminira wondered why she had hesitated to give King Luberto an answer immediately. Of course she would marry Prince Eadmund. He had asked her to stay and be fun. She would have a kingdom to rule with a husband that didn't care about her wealth and had no desire to rule her. Eadmund only cared that she laughed. That she was happy. That their lives be full of joy and fun. Laughter had been missing from her life for so long before she met him. Now, it was something she didn't want to part with, more precious than gold or jewels.

Aminira wondered where the Prince was. A canopied boat with a swan carved at the prow bobbed in the water and two servants waited on the boat, one at the rudder, one at the oars. Prince Eadmund had ordered the boat ready but wasn't present.

"You see, he is unreliable," Vizier Hamandir said as he strode up the planks of the dock, heels landing heavily on the weathered wood.

"Most men are," she said.

"Most men are not cursed without gravity."

"Gravity is becoming in only small doses. Most men drink far too much."

"You like him too much," the Vizier shot back. "I saw how you danced with him. What are you going to do?"

He sounded so desperate and a little sad, Aminira decided she would tell him all. She owed the ever loyal and ever concerned Vizier that much. Her news may not make him happy but eventually she hoped he would at least be glad that she was happy.

Before Aminira could utter a word, she heard her name called from the garden above the deck.

"Princess! Your Highness." Queen Gwinden ran down the garden path holding her skirts up to her knees to keep from tripping. A ladies maid, red faced and puffing, worked to keep up with Her Majesty.

Aminira's stomach knotted and her jaw clenched stubbornly. Maybe the queen was not so keen on King Luberto's match making. She may not want a foreign princess by her son's side.

The normally pale queen was grey faced despite her exertions and her hair, usually worn up, swung in a braid down her back. Aminira tensed, something was wrong, but it had to be worse than an unapproved marriage proposal.

Queen Gwinden came panting to a halt before Princess Aminira. She bent double, bracing her hands on her knees as she caught her breathe.

"Your Majesty," Aminira curtsied, and beside her the Vizier bowed low. "What is wrong?"

"You must come," the queen said. "My son...he asked for you." Tears spilled from her bloodshot eyes and ran down her sunken cheeks. Years of royal training and force of will kept her from sobbing.

"Please, Your Majesty, what has happened?" Aminira asked, her stomach suddenly a tight ball ready to expel what was left of her breakfast. Even as Aminira asked the queen what was wrong, she knew what it was.

Instead of the Queen, the maid behind her spoke up. "Prince Eadmund came back from swimming last night in a better humor than when he left. But he was more tired than usual. He ordered that boat there, and told me, you, Princess, were to meet him here on the morrow. Then he went to bed, but this morning he just kept sleeping. I tried to get him up, but he wouldn't wake. The king tried too, and the prince woke for a minute. He was delirious though, said the lake was dying, then went back to sleep."

"He woke again a few minutes ago," Queen Gwinden said, "He asked for the time, said he was late to meet you.

He tried to get up but he just sort of floated there, limp, and we put him back to bed. Please come."

"Of course," Aminira croaked before her throat squeezed shut.

As quickly as they could, Queen Gwinden and her servant ran back up the wide garden walks. Aminira followed behind, though she wanted to sweep past them at a dead run. However she didn't know the layout of the castle and she was forced to stay close to the queen.

Princess Yisabelle must be responsible for the prince's illness. The witch had done something. She had cursed Eadmund when he was a child and only she could alter the curse. Aminira wished she had put her dagger into Yisabelle's heart the night of the ball, though it may not have been enough to take the witch's life. Her hands curled into fists. There was always a way. Eadmund was alive. Curses could be broken. Witches could be slain. Aminira could save him. She would save him.

The queen charged into the castle, sending servants scattering. She ignored them, her grim focus on her son. They climbed a seemingly endless set of stairs and at the top was an open door. More servants milled in the room beyond, a gaggle of noble women who flocked to Queen Gwinden as she arrived on the landing, and even two of the doctors who Aminira recognized from her first luncheon at the palace hovered in the doorway.

Aminira pushed past them into the prince's rooms. He was in there, somewhere. Her head grew light and her heart pounded against her ribs. The crowd was silent and pensive. There was an air of a sick room, heavy and mournful, as if waiting for the patient to die. As if death was inevitable.

"Come, through here." Queen Gwinden, still breathless,

took Aminira's elbow and guided her through the sitting room to a chamber beyond. The queen pushed the door open and Aminira entered the prince's bedroom.

She thought her heart would stop. Prince Eadmund lay in a huge, four poster bed, a slim lump under light summer blankets. Resting on the blankets were sizable stones, none smaller than Aminira's fist, designed to keep Eadmund from floating out of bed. The weight of the blankets might have been enough but obviously no one was going to take the chance to lose the prince in his current condition.

"Go, you may talk to him." Queen Gwinden pointed a trembling finger then collapsed onto a chair next to her husband. Aminira hadn't noticed him before; the king was silent.

Swallowing the hard lump of fear in her throat, Aminira slowly approached the bed. The prince looked as if he might dry up and blow away.

"Your Highness?" Aminira's voice broke on the words. She coughed and tried again. "Prince Eadmund."

His eyes opened and he looked at her but she wasn't sure he really saw her. His gaze was dull. "My lake is dying," he whispered. "No reason to go out on it." His eyes focused on her at last. "Sorry." He rolled over and sank beneath the covers.

"Extreme melancholia," said a voice from the doorway.

Wu-Pei, the younger of the King's two hired philosophers, stood hands tucked in his sleeves. "Perhaps he will cry over the lake and break the curse."

"If not? What then?" Aminira asked thickly. The lump in her throat refused to leave.

"If the lake really does dry up, then his Highness' life is in danger. It is as we feared, the curse, the lake and the

Prince are tied to one another somehow," Wu-Pei said.

"Dying over a lake, fool boy," King Luberto said, his voice soft and warm and sad.

"Lakes don't just dry up. Do they?" Aminira looked over the room. Learned men, philosophers, doctors, all of them helplessly shuffling their feet. Useless.

"No, they don't," Wu-Pei said. "Not unless there is extreme drought."

"Or, they have help." Luberto's hand clenched into a fist and he pounded the arm of the chair. "It must be Yisabelle. She's gone too far this time."

"Drag her here in irons," Aminira said, almost shouting. How could everyone just stand around when only feet away, the prince lay dying?

"Don't you think I would if I could," Luberto shouted back, rising from his chair. Stalking over to Aminira, he stared her down. "What would you have me do against her magic?"

"Send me," Aminira said, meeting Luberto's eye and refusing to blink. "I can deal with a witch." Somewhere the Vizier coughed a polite warning but Aminira ignored him.

Luberto gestured to the room. "Out. All of you. I must talk with Princess Aminira."

The room froze for a moment, then the servants hustled out, followed by Wu-Pei and Hamandir.

Queen Gwinden hovered on the threshold a moment, face hard. "Tell her," she whispered just before shutting the doors of her son's bedroom.

"What?" Aminira asked the king. Luberto He sank into a chair with an exhausted wheeze, hands folded under his chin.

"Why do you hesitate? You must choose," Aminira said.

"Your sister or your son."

"Don't you think I know that," Luberto growled. "I told you Yisabelle has no heirs, didn't I?"

"Yes, but what has that to do with Prince Eadmund?"

"I'm the reason why. She was married off quite young, to a neighboring prince. A fool of a man who gave her a son before being beheaded by his brother in a palace coup. She fled back here, to Lagobel. I swore to raise the boy as my own, give them all the comforts they could ever want. I made the boy a duke and gave my sister her castle on the lake…" his voice choked off. The king let out a shaky sigh. "The boy, her son, my nephew, he died. He died while we were hunting. Gored by a wild boar. I was with him, it was on my watch. Yisabelle never forgave me. Maybe I-I never really forgave myself. She was always difficult, always magically talented, but after Dagren died she turned her back on the gods and embraced black magic. I know how she felt, why she did it. I was awaiting the birth of my firstborn when Dagren was killed. So I let her be. Left her to mourn. Even after she cursed my boy I let her be."

Aminira slumped against the bedroom wall. The only sound in the room was Eadmund's soft, even breathing. She understood, with awful clarity, King Luberto's impossible choice.

The Sultan, her father, had no son, so Aminira had been raised as the son he wanted. But his wife, Aminira's mother, had died when Aminira was a child. By law, the Sultan could have but one heir. Even his concubines were forbidden children. With only a daughter, the Sultan, who in his mercy had refused to kill his younger brother, designated her uncle Maudood as future Sultan.

All would have been well had the Sultan not remarried.

Her father's second wife was with child. If the child was a boy the Sultan would have his heir and her Uncle Maudood would be executed. Unless Maudood could assassinate the Sultan before that happened. Maudood had already come to Aminira, asking her help, promising she would be a ruler in her own right, perhaps governor of the richest provinces in Qadhar, or even general of her Uncle's armies. If only she would side with him.

She could not. She would not choose between her father and her uncle. And she couldn't stand to stay in Qadhar only to witness Maudood's death. Or her own. If the Sultan fell and she was not on Maudood's side he would execute her as well.

Aminira had begged her father to let her leave. Let her go to the Northlands, across the ocean, marry a foreign prince, become the queen she would never be in Qadhar. The Sultan knew how precarious her position in court was and he released her with his blessing.

But even in the north, her father and the brewing storm back home was ever on her mind. The impossible choice of family over family was the same as Luberto's. Who to choose? Father or uncle? Sister or son?

She had fled once. Could she bring herself to leave again? Eadmund rolled over in his sleep. He smiled, perhaps dreaming of the lake. Aminira wanted to hear him laugh again. Wanted him to spring out of bed and ask to be flown like a kite. If only he did that, this second, she would agree. Her eyes stung and she rubbed them. If she wasn't going to leave him, then she had to save him.

"The curse has changed. And it is Princess Yisabelle who has changed it. It must be. Unless a new witch has come," Aminira whispered.

"I know that," Luberto balled his fist and drove it into the arm of the chair. "Don't you think I know?"

"I understand the pain of this. More than you might think. But Princess Yisabelle has forced your hand. You must choose."

"My son," Luberto said, voice breaking. He stared at the bed, eyes wet and unfocused. "Save him and Lagobel is yours."

"If I save Prince Eadmund," Aminira said, "then I will marry him. Provided he'll have me."

"Go, go tell them," the king gestured towards the door but didn't move to leave his seat.

Aminira threw her shoulders back. She gave Eadmund a final look, then pushed open the bedroom door. The crowd beyond turned as one. She felt their eyes on her, the queen desperate. Hamandir scrutinized her with his usual disapproval, a shadow of fear haunting his eyes. The rest, waited to see what the verdict would be.

"I am going to see Princess Yisabelle and demand she lift her curse. May Almighty Re-Hurakh help her if she does not." Amanira touched her forehead and gestured skyward to the unseen sun.

The Vizier let out a choking noise as he held back a litany of complaints which Aminira would have to listen to later. She didn't care. He could protest all he wanted. Her heart was firm.

"Oh, my dear." Queen Gwinden rushed to Princess Aminira, sweeping her up in a fierce hug. Aminira felt the queen trembling.

Unfamiliar emotions battered at Aminira's resolve not to cry, but she held on. Hope and belonging. Neither of which she'd felt in ages. Perhaps her mother had once hugged her, may God keep her, as this queen did now. The acute emotions mixed and bled together, and rising from them, if she dared admit it...emerged love. The cynical voices of her father and uncle whispered she was getting a kingdom out of the deal, but she didn't care. Not now that she could lose Eadmund. Without him, she didn't want Lagobel. The thought of losing him sickened her and she pushed away her fears as she returned the queen's unexpected embrace.

Gwinden let her go. Aminira thought the woman might burst into tears, an event she was even less prepared for than the hug. But the queen's tears hovered on the surface of her eyes, sparkling in the summer light coming in through the window. She smiled as she let go of Aminira.

"Are you sure? Will you really? Will you be alright?"

Not trusting her voice, Aminira bowed to the queen. She wasn't sure if or when she had ever been so welcome. She hadn't even saved Prince Eadmund. Yisabelle could destroy her yet. But for the barest moment, Aminira let herself feel accepted by a family she never anticipated having. Aminira squared her shoulders and hardened herself. "I must go prepare myself."

With that, she turned to leave. She gestured curtly at Hamandir as she walked past him.

The instant the carriage horses took up their trot, the Vizier could keep silent no longer.

"What are you thinking? You're actually going to fight a witch for some boy you've barely met? Prince or no, kingdom or no, this is madness."

"I met the prince my first night in Lagobel when I was

lost in the woods. I found the lake and Prince Eadmund."

"The first night?" Vizier Hamandir sputtered. A familiar vein throbbed on his forehead. "What have you been doing together all this time?"

Aminira glared imperiously at the Vizier and he shrank back a little in the carriage seat.

"We have gone swimming together and danced at the ball. That is all," she replied once she felt Hamandir looked chastened enough.

"I swore to your father I would protect you. How am I to do that if you will not listen to reason?"

"Regardless, I am going to confront Yisabelle. I am going to save him and you cannot stop me. I would much rather you were on my side."

The Vizier's scowl deepened and he looked at the floor of the carriage. "I am on your side, always," he said at last, voice barely audible over the rattle of wheels and the clip clop of the horses' hooves. "But truly. This is the prince you wish to marry?"

"He is," Aminira said.

After a long silence the Vizier said, "Very well."

The carriage rattled into the inn's courtyard. Aminira stepped out before the Vizier and spotted Bea across the yard exercising one of the camels. It trailed docile on its lead.

Bea smiled and waved when she spotted Aminira. She glanced around, making sure the lead groom was out of sight and pulled the camel over.

"Your Highness." The girl bowed. Aminira saw Bea's grin

dissolve into concern and realized how grim she must look.

Aminira tried to smile at the girl but her face felt tight. She quit trying and said, "Leave off the camel and attend me."

Bea nodded and took the beast back to the barn.

"Unpack what I need to confront a witch," she told the Vizier. "I'll be in my room."

"Yes, Your Highness," he said and went to talk to the wagon master.

A second later, Bea dashed across the courtyard. She stopped in front of Aminira, worry wrinkling her young face.

"What happened?" Bea asked. "What about the prince?"

"Come." Aminira turned and went inside.

When they reached her suite she dismissed all the servants and left orders that only the Vizier be permitted to see her.

Alone with Bea, Aminira dropped onto a couch. Head in her hands, she shut her eyes and tried to breath. The vision of Eadmund lying in bed rose behind her eyes. He'd looked so indifferent. Even the brief smile that came with his apology had no energy or life behind it.

Bea touched Aminira's back and tried to soothe her. She opened her eyes and straightened up.

"Did Prince Eadmund say no? He couldn't have, could he?" Beas asked.

"I will tell you, but first you must promise, as a loyal subject of King Luberto and as my friend, to tell no one else," Aminira said.

Bea solemnly crossed her heart with her index finger. "I swear to the gods."

"The Prince is dying."

Bea gasped and wobbled a moment before sitting on the floor. "He can't be."

"It is the curse. Something has changed. Prince Eadmund says the lake is drying up. His life seems tied to the lake in a way no one understands."

"No," Bea said stubbornly. "He can't die. You're going to marry him and stay here forever."

"I will try, Bea," Aminira said. Why was she worrying the girl with her problems? Bea was only thirteen. Despite living alone on the streets, starving and scraping for anything of use, she still had faith. In what, Aminira could not imagine, but that faith seemed to have settled on Aminira. And somehow, Bea was her friend. Her only friend. One that had shared her romance, such as it was, with Prince Eadmund, since the very first night. Bea had encouraged her, had believed in all the silly stories that ended with the prince and princess getting married and living happily ever after. In so many ways Bea had far more faith than Aminira who knew that life usually ended in loss and blood.

"Can I help?" Bea asked. "What will break the curse? How do we save him?"

"First I must confront Princess Yisabelle."

"The witch?" Bea scrambled to her feet. "But what if she kills you?"

"Do you think I would do such a thing if I didn't have the means to fight her?"

"You do magic? Really?"

"No. But I know how to fight it. Witches such as Her Highness are not tolerated in Qadhar. Any who use their power to curse another person are put to death."

A knock at the door interrupted Aminira and the Vizier

stepped in. He carried two matching wooden cases with him, one long, the other square. Both were carved of ebony and inlaid with mother of pearl. Bea's eyes widened when she saw the cases. The Vizier glared at the girl and set them down before Aminira with great care, as if the contents might shatter. Aminira knelt on the floor in front of the long case and traced her finger reverently over the iridescent inlay. The case vibrated beneath her fingertip like the heartbeat of a bird, so fast it was a hum.

The vibration fluttered and stilled as if something inside waited, breath held. In a way it was true. Aminira counted the inlaid tiles, five in from the left hand star and six from the right edge. She pressed the tile and felt a mechanism release.

Now the case could be safely opened. Aminira lifted the lid. Inside nestled in a velvet lined hollow rested a curved long sword. The silver sheath was set with fiery rubies, garnets, and topaz.

Bea inhaled sharply, taking in the jewels and silver with glittering eyes.

"Touch the hilt," Aminira said.

"Can I?" Bea asked.

"Yes."

Bea touched the sword's hilt with a newly calloused finger. She yanked it back. "It's warm."

"The blade contains the soul of an Ifrit, a female Djinn, and their souls are made of fire. Only a woman may wield it, which is why my father let me take the sword. It can cut through spells and defend the bearer from magic."

"You really can save Prince Eadmund."

"Of course she can," Vizier Hamandir snapped. "Our princess is a great warrior."

The Vizier had not shown so much faith in the carriage on the way back to the inn. Aminira almost reminded him of that, but Bea didn't seem upset by his outburst. She nodded her agreement.

"What's in the other case then?" she asked. "They match."

"These are more witch hunting tools." Aminira pulled the ebony box over. It opened much like the sword case, its mechanisms hidden in the inlaid mosaic. Aminira pressed two tiles on the side, felt the click and pushed a third tile on the front. The lid opened smoothly. "These are simpler tools than Ifrit, designed to defend me from magic."

Princess Aminira pulled out each item and showed them to Bea who gazed at each one with wide eyed eagerness.

"Kohl dissolved in holy oil. Paint it around your eyes and you can see through illusions. These gold bracers are etched with protection spells." Aminira turned the gold bracers so they caught the light just right. The spells, written in the ancient language of the long dead Zaso, glowed faintly. "And last, an amulet that wards off evil spirits, should the witch have any in her thrall." She pulled out a velvet drawstring bag and opened it. Nestled in the black velvet was a carved lapis pendant. A mystical 'hand' with three fingers and two short 'thumbs' on either side. An eye of moonstone and lapis looked up, unblinking, from the palm of the amulet. Smaller cobalt glass eyes hung from the chain, strung between gold discs etched with geometric seals.

The amulet had been in her family for generations, said to have been crafted by the great magi Nashara two hundred years ago. Its effectiveness against magic, like Ifrit, had been proven time and again. Sadly it could not break a curse already cast. None of the relics in her possession could cure, they could fend off magic attacks and prevent curses from taking hold. Which meant they could not lift Eadmund's affliction, but they would protect Aminira whatever dark magic Yisabelle could hurl at her.

"Can I come with you? I know how to fight, I learned on the streets" Bea asked, eyes aglow with wonder.

"It's too dangerous," Aminira said. "I will be going alone."

"Surely not?" Vizier Hamandir added.

"I can risk no one else and these are all the weapons we have."

"King Luberto may have some trained soldiers, one of their priests even," the Vizier argued.

Bea pursed her lips. "I used to hang around the Abby of Gerulfus, hoping to see a witch hunter." Bea must have seen the question writ on Aminira's face because she said, "Gerulfus is the God of knowledge and learning, protector of white magic. The witch hunters all belong to His order. I saw a witch hunter once, years ago. They travel far and wide to fight black magic. Too many evil witches and not enough hunters I guess. If we don't have a witch hunter right here, right now, it'll take a while to get one."

The Vizier grunted with frustration. "Your Highness, I must object again. None of this need be your concern. Let the prince's family deal with their own mess."

"No," Bea turned to the Vizier. "Princess Aminira loves Prince Eadmund. In the stories, the hero always saves their beloved and lives happily ever after."

"This is not a story. You know nothing. You're little more than an impudent child." The Vizier's hand rose, ready to strike her. Bea braced herself for the blow but stared defiantly up at the Vizier.

"Stop it, both of you," Aminira commanded and he froze. "You are both my dear friends and there is no need to fight."

With a soul deep sigh of disgust that conveyed the Vizier's feelings on the subject of Bea, Aminira's recent decisions, and indeed, the world itself, he lowered his hand.

"I know you both want the best for me. But, at a certain point you must allow that I know my own heart. Bea, real life is not like a story. What I undertake is dangerous and there is a chance that I may not return. If that happens you are welcome to go with my people back to Qadarh and become a camel keeper. And, Hamandir, you will see to her comfort and security.

"To both of you, I say, I was trained by my father, Sultan Caylim, who is a great warrior. Hamandir, you could use a little of Bea's faith in me. I am well armed, and well prepared. Princess Yisabelle will not have an easy time trying to kill me."

Silent, Bea nodded and sat back down.

The muscles in Hamandir's jaw strained as he bit back whatever it looked like he wanted to say. At last he came out with, "What do you need me to do?"

"Send King Luberto a message. I need a boat and boatmen ready at dawn to take me to Yisabelle's castle. Ask also if he has anyone who can fight magic. Another witch or witch hunter who could accompany me. In any case, I leave at dawn."

"Very well, Your Highness," Vizier Hamandir bowed to her and left.

When he was gone, Bea threw her arms around Aminira in a tight hug. Surprised, Aminira froze. She felt Bea shaking like a palm tree swayed by desert winds. The girl smelled warmly of the stables, sweet hay, earthy dung, and the musk of camels.

Aminira relaxed enough to pat Bea on the back and realized that this was the second time in one day she had been embraced. Something that had never happened before in her life. She put her arms around Bea and held her friend close.

CHAPTER 10

Sunlight had not yet touched the rippled surface of the lake but Aminira could see the water was indeed lower than it had been the day before. The blackish waters were well below the lime-white crust of the lowest watermark.

Last night, King Luberto had informed Vizier Hamandir that he had no fighters trained against magic. He had always feared Yisabelle would take it as a sign of hostility and finish off Prince Eadmund once and for all. A fear he now bitterly regretted. And Yisabelle's reputation had kept any white magic witches from taking up residence on Lagobel. The boat and rowers however, he could easily provide.

When Princess Aminira had arrived at the Royal dock before sunrise, the boat and its attendants were waiting with another missive from the King.

Prince Eadmund's mood had worsened. He pined for his lake, refusing all food and company. He had demanded to be left alone and would not leave his bed. The curse too was spreading. Word had come from across the lake that two of the rivers which fed the waters, were now trickles, hardly fit to be called a stream.

Aminira looked over the side of the boat. If all the water in the kingdom dried up, Lagobel would die along with its prince. The lush forests, reduced to tinder, fields left to bake and harden. The people would leave and Lagobel would be a wasteland. She silently recited the cants of protection.

Her hand tightened on the warm hilt of Ifrit and Aminira glared at where she thought Yisabelle's castle was. The witch would soon find her arrogance repaid with justice.

"Can you row faster?" she asked, anxious to confront the witch. The rowers picked up their pace and the air moved faster against her face. Today she wore no head scarf, her hair instead, tucked under a padded cowl topped with a chainmail hood and a pointed helm atop that. Toughened leather and chainmail covered everything but her hands and face. On her wrists glowed the gold bracers, their faint protection spells occasionally picking up the pink of the lightening pre-dawn sky.

The rugged coastline of the lake drew closer and the boat rounded an island dotted horn of land. Beyond loomed Princess Yisabelle's castle, the stones stained black, the green witch lights faint.

A decaying dock hung over the water, the wooden supports grey and dry. She pointed at the dock even though there was nowhere else for the boat to put in. Only sheer rock and masonry met the water along this stretch of shore.

The oarsman pulled the boat alongside a ladder that would normally have been partially submerged. The final rung dangled just above the side of the boat. Princess Aminira climbed out and stood for a moment on the dock.

"If I do not return by sunset, I am dead," she told the rowers. "Wait here until then. Go tell the king if I do not return."

"Aye Highness," one man said for both. They boatmen nodded and bowed but she saw the nervous knot of their brows and hoped their courage held out. Aminira turned and left the dock.

Rickety stairs led up to a wide landing cut out of rock. Aminira saw the shadow of a door set into the foundation of the castle. Once it had been used, no doubt, to welcome guests visiting by boat. Now lichen and moss sprouted from deep cracks in the rock.

Princess Aminira kept close to the castle stones as she ascended and drew Ifrit from her scabbard a few steps from the door. Careful and fully expecting a trap to spring at any moment, Aminira stepped onto the landing.

Nothing happened. The iron bound oak door into the castle had rotted away, the weathered grey planks splintered and laced with holes.

Was Princess Yisabelle really so arrogant? Perhaps. She had lived, free and untroubled in her brother's kingdom since her exile from her previous home. Maybe she assumed no one would ever come for her.

Aminira kept Ifrit unsheathed anyway. The lax security could be part of a trap. Yisabelle could be daring the unwary to enter. With a booted foot Aminira kicked in the door. The weak spots shattered and the rusted iron bindings clanged to the ground.

Beyond was a dark and dusty reception hall swathed in cobwebs. High narrow windows, their glass filthy, let in grayish light. Aminira tensed and crossed the threshold, again expecting a trap of some kind. Again there was nothing.

She exhaled but knew it too early to grow complacent. Yisabelle had the power to drain a lake. She commanded great magic. Just because she relied on reputation to repel visitors and thieves, did not mean Aminira would have an easy confrontation with the princess.

Her booted footfalls were softened by the thick carpet of dust and, even inside, the moss and lichen continued to thrive. Aminira moved carefully, as silently as she could, though she wished she had not traded her silk slippers for Northern style boots.

On the far side of the hall, a broad staircase climbed into the castle, leading to the main floors. Five or six people could easily walk abreast up the stairs. Aminira pictured the former grandeur of the hall. It was a shame only spiders and rodents enjoyed it now.

Back to the wall, Aminira ascended. Her plan was to catch Yisabelle unaware. Sleeping or at breakfast. Give the witch no time to prepare her spells in advance. But, Aminira was beginning to think she'd spend most of the day searching the castle for the woman.

No one passed her on the stairs. The only foot prints disturbing the dust were her own. No sound came from above or below. Was Yisabelle even at home? Aminira hadn't thought her plan might fail because the witch had simply left.

She fought the urge to call out just to see if there was a reply. A guard or servant would be a welcome sight, reassurance that Yisabelle was in residence.

The stairs ended at an even grander hall than the reception room below. Columns forested the cavernous space, their carved floral capitals home to nesting birds which came and went through shattered stained glass windows, their droppings streaked the pillars white.

Did the Princess really live like this? She could have been living in luxury provided by her brother. Instead she had let the castle rot and crumble. Maybe she only needed a few rooms for her arcane work, but still, why forego comfort for this? If Aminira had not worn the holy oil around her eyes would she see the castle differently?

Aminira hugged the wall looking for doors and still wary of attack, though that seemed less and less likely.

Toward the front of the room was an empty dais built presumably for a throne. Decorative arches on either side of the great hall led to darkened corridors. The left half, if Aminira's bearings were correct, led to the outer wall and probably the landward entrance to the castle. She turned right, heading deeper into the bizarre emptiness.

More deserted corridors and empty rooms with decaying tapestries and the skeletal remains of unidentifiable furniture met her. She passed through a dining room built for huge parties, a long splintered wood table lining its center. Rodent paw prints and tail marks mapped out trails in the dusty floor.

A small group of mice scurried from a passageway hidden behind a decorative column. A fat, brown mother rat quickly herding her children followed the mice seconds later.

They were leaving somewhere, fleeing from the deeper regions of the castle. Families and nests forced out by something. Maybe Yisabelle's magic or the lack of water.

Aminira headed down the passageway. It was wide, but close, unlit and without the luxury of windows. She touched a ruby on Ifrit's hilt and the blade glowed with golden light. There were more mice and rats scurrying away in the corridor along with weirder and vastly out of place residents.

Blind, whitish-brown crickets scuttled along the walls and floor, their long feelers testing the air. Her footsteps crunched. Aminira took back every bad thought she'd had about the uncomfortable boots. She was just grateful her voluminous pants were already tucked into the top of the heavy leather and the laces tight.

High pitched squeaks, almost above hearing, warned her of the bats swooping along the ceiling. Their ammonia rich droppings hadn't had time to build up so this migration of rats, mice, crickets, and bats were recent.

At last the corridor opened into a long, low kitchen faintly illuminated by morning sun pushing through small, dirty windows. There were half a dozen ovens, all built for different purposes; one a huge blackened maw big enough for an entire deer carcass to turn on a spit. Bread ovens and smaller ovens with iron racks, and spits for fowl. Stoves, sinks, and huge islands of scarred butcher blocks broke up the space.

And here, the only signs of habitation Aminira had come across. Drying herbs hung from ceiling hooks, lidded crock jars, shiny with use lined a set of shelves next to more arcane ingredients floating in glass jars. Beetles crawled along the shelves and a countless number churned in the sink, trapped by the smooth metal sides, unable to climb out. The remnants of a meal, left on the kitchen table, was being scavenged by a huge black cat.

Yisabelle lived here then, ignoring the rest of the castle and confining herself to the heart, the kitchen. No servants or guards to wait on her. Then where was she?

Aminira waded further into the kitchen. Yisabelle

couldn't be far. She must have a bed chamber; there was nowhere to sleep unless she laid herself on cold stone. And somewhere must be a workshop for her dark arts.

Something feather light, like spider silk, touched Aminira's cheek and she brushed it away. A cobweb, perhaps. Then she heard a moan, soft, low and agonized, growing louder.

The room darkened, shadows thickening into oily iridescent pools. Inside the shadow pools, forms swirled, writhing and twining, slithering over each other like a barrel of eels. Things, not quite human, rose from the well of darkness, bodies made of writhing snakes. The figures growled and hissed, their voices caught between pain and rage.

Aminira's lip curled. The first test of her protections was an easy one. Though more than enough to send the average thief screaming into the night, the apparitions closing in on her were illusions.

The holy oil painted around her eyes worked. As dreadful as the visions that menaced her were, they were transparent. Beyond them Aminira could see the unchanged kitchen. The apparitions couldn't touch or affect anything physical. They shambled closer, limbs snaking toward her.

She swung Ifrit in a graceful arc and the monsters dissolved as the sword cut the air they occupied.

A derisive snort echoed through the cold kitchen. Aminira's head whipped around, searching for the source. On the far side of the kitchen a lurked shaded alcove. Yisabelle peeled away from the wall. Her simple grey dress blended with the murk so well Aminira had not seen her. How long had she been watching?

"So, you came," Yisabelle said, emphasis on 'you', not

surprised but pleased. Her mouth twisted in a frown-smile, jagged, brittle, and humorless.

"Yes," Aminira said. She tried to edge closer to Yisabelle without looking like she was moving. There was no way to run directly at Yisabelle, too many tables and work stations blocked the way. By the time she was across the room, Yisabelle could attack her in any number of ways.

Yisabelle's eyes flashed red in the gloom and Aminira knew the witch was also gauging the distance between them. Aminira calculated several ways across the kitchen judging the best places that offered cover. A fight in the kitchen could drag out and Aminira wondered if she could lure Yisabelle away.

The witch raised her hand and made slashing motions with her finger. Arcs of green flame, small at first, flew toward Aminira, gathering speed and size. They cut through the hanging herbs, scattering pungent leaves, and sending the seething mass of beetles into a panic.

Aminira raised Ifrit, instinctively slicing through the green flare which came too fast to dodge. The fire burst apart and a cold—so intense Aminira's face and hands went numb—exploded around her. She dropped and rolled beneath a table, barely missing the second flame. It hit the other end of the kitchen, splashing like water but freezing as it hit. The stones of the wall cracked with the sudden temperature change.

Ifrit steamed in Aminira's hand and she thanked Almighty God that the sword was blessed with fire. It was all that saved her.

She peered between the legs of the table to see if Yisabelle still lay in wait. Aminira could just see a slice of alcove. It was empty. The witch could still be there, sheltered or hiding just out of sight. Aminira needed to attack. She couldn't hide under a table forever.

Keeping her head down, Aminira raised Ifrit's blade above the table. Using the blade as a mirror, she scouted the kitchen. Nothing. Yisabelle had retreated. Aminira sprang from behind the table and crossed the rest of the kitchen, quick as a gazelle. So much for luring the witch into the open. Now Aminira was forced to follow Yisabelle's dance.

The alcove sheltered three doors. The first led to a washroom, the second to a pantry, the third to broad stairs spiraling into yet more darkness. Aminira ignored the pantry. Yisabelle could escape through the washroom, as it likely had access to the lake. But the old witch was patient and bold. She had cursed her nephew and stayed for years to watch him. Aminira doubted that Yisabelle would leave even now that Luberto had finally sent someone after her. Not if she wanted to see the end results of her curse.

Like an omen, a ghostly translucent centipede climbed from whatever pit the stairs lead to. Hugging the central column, Aminira made her way down, Ifrit aloft and lighting the way.

The staircase was shorter than Aminira thought, their wide curve terminating in a spacious wine cellar. The wine was long since gone and only a few crumbling oak casks home to shiny black roaches remained.

Yisabelle was nowhere in sight but that didn't mean she'd disappeared in a flash of magic. There was a crack in the far wall—a straight crack—from which a cluster of cave crickets escaped, their spiky legs clinging to the brickwork. A hidden door leading to… what? Aminira had to find out. Either Yisabelle would be behind it or Aminira had lost the witch.

Wary, sword poised to strike in case Yisabelle leapt out of the nowhere, Aminira headed for the cellar wall. A snap echoed suddenly in the musty air, and Aminira froze. Beneath her boot something broke in half.

She looked down and saw a delicate white bone. The floor was littered with them. So thick with dirt and cobwebs, they looked like part of an uneven floor, though now she knew what she was looking for, Aminira could make out a mix of bones. Small and large, some big enough to be human, some larger that could have come from game animals or oxen.

The bones shivered all across the floor, shaking the dirt off. Puffs of dust rose from the bones as they began to assemble themselves.

Merciful God! Yisabelle had led her right into a trap. Bone upon bone locked together, their order chaotic as a nightmare. Arms made of spines formed, nimble fingers tipped in sharp-toothed rodent skulls. Human remains mixed with dog and cat bones, making a multiheaded body bristling with ribs.

A needle-edged whip of snake and fish bones thrust from the monster's hand. It slashed across her mailed cowl and sliced open her cheek. Aminira called on Ifrit's fiery spirit and the blade danced with orange flames. She cut diagonally across the monster's body.

The bones fell apart, a few of them burned to ash. Then they reassembled, slightly different this time. The dog skull with its sharp ivory teeth twisted on a long neck of thick cow vertebrae that rose higher than Aminira's head.

She struck again. The dry, twiggy snap of breaking bones echoed in the cellar. Aminira cut in half a cat skull, several ribs, and obliterated a small complete mouse skeleton that turned to powder with the force of Ifrit.

Again, the creature simply rearranged itself. The monster lashed out quick and low with a flail made of heavy thigh bones. Aminira was swept off her feet and thrown against the brick wall. Pain throbbed through her as she rolled to her feet. Nothing felt broken but Aminira knew there would be deep bruises.

So far, Yisabelle's monster hadn't done much damage. But fighting it was taking too long, wearing her out. She needed to destroy more bones. If she could take them all out with one blow, the monster would have nothing left to assemble itself with.

Aminira clutched Ifrit, her back to the wall, as the bone creature approached again. This time the arms were spinal columns ending in dog skulls, its body a mass of broken deer antlers ready to impale her if she came within reach.

Ifrit had one more power which Aminira had hoped to save for Yisabelle. The blade created fireballs of tremendous strength which burned even underwater. But there was a limit to how many the blade could produce before Ifrit needed to rest. If she exhausted the blade, she'd be armed with a regular sword.

The monster feinted left and Aminira tried to parry, but a hidden appendage sprung from its chest and wrapped around her sword arm. Mismatched vertebrae squeezed, crushing her wrist and Aminira cried out. The bones moved up her arm trying to find purchase on the gold bracer.

The bracer flashed with light and the monster recoiled, the bones that had touched her dissolved to powder.

Her sword arm was free again and nothing broken, but her wrist throbbed with pain. Aminira changed hands.

She had been trained to use a sword with either, though her left was weaker.

She called up Ifrit's power and the flaming blade became an inferno.

The bones, as if knowing what was coming, dropped to the floor and scattered, inert once more. Aminira's lip curled. That wouldn't save them. Fire gathered at the tip of Ifrit's blade, a growing sphere like a miniature sun. As long as Aminira held the sword she couldn't feel the flames and they couldn't harm her.

When the fireball was as big as her head, Aminira pointed Ifrit at the floor and unleashed the fire. It exploded against the stone and spread in a wave, the flood rippled out and crashed against the walls. Everything on the floor was consumed in the conflagration. Old barrels blazed bright, collapsed and died in the flame.

A few of the bones tried to escape the roiling flames. They rose from the lake of fire, trailing smoke and embers as they fell to ash.

The tide of fire ebbed and then extinguished leaving the cellar floor glazed black. Heat rippled off the cooling stones but Aminira couldn't feel it, not with Ifrit's protection. She cut the hem off her robe and bound her wrist, then slid the bracer down her arm for extra support. It would have to do. This was a magical battle anyway; were it down to just swords, Aminira had every confidence she could cut an old woman down left handed. However, brute force would not win her the Eadmund's safety.

Aminira cautiously made her way to the crack in the cellar wall. She slid Ifrit through, hoping the sword could sever any enchantments waiting for her. Nothing happened. No monster emerged from the brickwork, no unearthly screams rang out. Aminira tugged at the crack and felt the wall give. She pulled harder and a small section of the wall, barely wide enough for a single person to slip through, opened up.

A narrow staircase, steep and cut from native stone plunged into the earth. Water dripped from the ceiling creating stalagmites and feeding a glowing blue fungus that clung to the stone. The faint light wasn't enough to see the bottom and Aminira couldn't tell where or if the stairs ended. But somewhere down there Yisabelle must be waiting.

The damp walls brushed Aminira's shoulders as she descended and her injured wrist pulsed with every heartbeat. Minutes ticked by measured by her footfalls on the stone. She came across grazing crickets and glassy spiders that fed on them. Maybe the stairs themselves were an endless trap and she'd never reach the bottom.

Aminira stopped walking. She touched the amulet around her neck and sang the blessed cant of protection, used only in the direst of circumstances. The amulet grew hot then shockingly cold in her hand. The blue fungal light dimmed then brightened as a ripple passed along the walls of the narrow passage. Her ears popped. When the light returned to its even glow, she pushed on. The powerful magics Yisabelle had used on the corridor hopefully broken. It must have been a strong ward of some kind, had it been an illusion she would have seen past it.

A quarter of an hour passed as Aminira descended, the only life she encountered were cave insects and roosting bats. Had she picked the wrong passage after all? Aminira was tempted to turn back, try the laundry room. She kept picturing Yisabelle escaping across the lake, but that didn't feel quite right.

Then Aminira caught a whiff of a familiar smell. Lake water. The cool, rich scent drifted up the stairs mixing with the sharp scent of bat droppings. Another twenty steps down and Aminira felt a draft on her face.

She hurried as much as she dared on the slippery stone, down and down, until she saw a gap in the stone at the bottom of the stairs. She crouched down and peered out to see what lay beyond. She gasped.

A huge cavern lit with the same blue glow as the stairs opened up so vast the great distance of its horizon was lost in darkness. Huge stalagmites, sharp and round as a jackal's teeth, hung from the ceiling. Some had joined their twin stalactite growing from below, forming pillars. The cavern floor was flooded and Aminira heard the roar of a waterfall.

Waterfall wasn't the right word though. A column of churning water poured into the cavern, unimaginable gallons a minute. The lake itself drained into the cave. Aminira blinked, numb with shock. The massive cataract was not alone. Rivers gushed down the walls to fill the cave. All the water in the kingdom was disappearing here.

"Come out, princess." Yisabelle's voice echoed in the cavern. "Come see what I have done."

Aminira straightened up and edged sideways through the narrow break in the rock.

Yisabelle waited a few feet away, her eyes blue-green, the color somehow smug.

"I'm glad Luberto sent you," Yisabelle said.

"He didn't send me. I came on my own with his blessing," Aminira said.

"No doubt." Yisabelle nodded. "You are, after all, the author of my nephew's recent happiness."

"He's always happy," Aminira replied evenly, though her

stomach tightened with sickening knowledge.

"Ah, but I know how to read the waters. Lightness of being is not true happiness. He knows no contrast. But love… that has weight. And his deepens just a bit everyday you're here."

"The philosophers are right. His life is tied to the lake," Aminira said.

"Certainly took them long enough to figure it out, didn't it?" Yisabelle waved a hand, sounding bored.

"But why kill him now? Why kill the whole kingdom?" Aminira demanded. She raised her sword as much to look threatening as to put a weapon between herself and Yisabelle.

"You have to ask? Didn't dear Luberto tell you the whole tragic tale before sending you after me?"

"This will not bring your son back."

"No, but it's all Luberto deserves," Yisabelle's hands clenched into fists. "He was supposed to safeguard Dagren. He swore it to me when we fled. Dagren should have been king. Should have been the eldest legitimate heir to the throne. But Luberto couldn't stand it. He let my son die so his could have Lagobel." Yisabelle's eyes turned black as she spewed her hatred. "But I have won. There will be no Lagobel."

"Stop this. Put an end to the curse or—"

"Or what?" Yisabelle shouted, advancing a step. "You'll kill me? It won't make a difference. You can't stop this, not now."

Aminira retreated as Yisabelle came at her, expecting another magical attack. The witch only grin-grimaced. Her upper lip curled into an amused snarl.

The sound of the waters changed. The steady roar broken

by the churning of white water. Aminira saw something bubble and rise in the distance. The waves along the artificial shore where she stood rose higher, lapping over her boots as tiny whitecaps formed.

The surface heaved as something immense almost breached, receded, then launched itself at the shore fast as an arrow. Aminira had the impression of something lithe and undulating. Ifrit began building another fireball at its tip.

As the thing reached the shore, the waters broke, pouring off black skin speckled with glowing yellow spots. A gaping mouth big enough to swallow a village whole filled Aminira's vision. The thing was part eel, part snake, fleshy, scaled, all teeth and mouth, and cold blooded death. She aimed Ifrit, not caring if the fireball was ready. She needed to strike the monster before it could swallow her.

Aiming down the eel's black maw, Aminira released the mystical flames. But the eel snapped its mouth shut and ducked. A wall of flesh, a finned tail flat and solid as a brick wall, rose up and flicked Aminira aside. The fireball flew wide and hit the ceiling scorching the blue fungus.

The ferocious blow from the eel snake's tail hit like a boulder, knocking the air from Aminira's lungs. She flew through the air until she was stopped by the uneven stone wall of the cavern. Ridges of rock dug into her and every bone in her body jarred painfully. Aminira tumbled to the floor, an immobile heap of agony.

Yisabelle's hysterical laughter cut through the roar of water, echoing in Aminira's ears. She had to move before the eel-snake struck again, but first she had to breathe again. Pain tore through Aminira's chest as she sucked in air forcing, her to sip when she needed to gulp.

She forced herself to her knees in time to see the eel-snake lunge again. Aminira rolled to the side and it barely missed her. The monster's cold, fetid breath choked her.

Ifrit was still her best hope to kill the monster and Yisabelle but she had maybe two more fire balls left at her disposal before the sword could make more. She had to hit the eel-snake and hit it fast or she'd be the next morsel to disappear down its gullet.

Aminira pushed to her feet and silently ordered Ifrit to form another fireball. A few feet away, Yisabelle stood sheltered in the monsters coils. Its broad, flat tail protected her and she stroked its back scales.

The witch's eyes flashed emerald and the creature lunged again, the coils of its body springing forward in a smooth and deadly arc. Aminira brought up Ifrit aiming for the soft spotted folds of the monster's throat.

The fireball streaked like a blinding comet through the air, its aim true. The magical flame hit and spread along the eel-snake's body. With a hissing cry the fiend reeled back and plunged into the water. Aminira's eyes watered as the rancid stench the eel left behind hit her. She had smelled burning flesh and cooking eel before but this was neither.

She strode toward the princess; the witch now bereft of her pet monster. Aminira hoped Yisabelle would be shaken after the eel-snake's retreat but the witch stood firm, letting Aminira get closer and closer.

It must be another trap. Aminira asked Ifrit for one more fireball. The sword obliged but she could feel that this would be the last one. It had to count.

The dark lake water exploded as the eel-snake surfaced, shedding droplets and wetting Aminira. Yisabelle's frown-smile stretched with triumph. As the eel rose, Aminira saw what little damage Ifrit's fire had inflicted on the beast. The smooth skin of its neck was burned and blistered but the wound was superficial. Its unblinking yellow eyes fixed on Aminira and she saw her death between the long daggers of its teeth.

With a hiss louder than the falling water, the eel-snake dove at Aminira again. She watched, frozen, terrified as the pinkish-grey spike like maw opened to swallow her. From far away she heard Yisabelle's cruel laughter. The witch was sure of victory and for a heartbeat; Aminira believed she'd lost as well.

In a flash, Aminira saw a way out of death even as the monster's mouth filled her world. She brought the sword up, keeping it close to her body, and with a thought commanded more fire from Ifrit. The blade burned inches from her face though she could not feel the fire.

Aminira held fast as the jaws closed around her. A sob of terror escaped her but still she didn't move. The rancid breath of the beast choked her.

It snapped its mouth shut and Aminira screamed as one of the eel-snake's fangs stabbed her thigh, the curved sickle of tooth drove into her flesh only stopping when it hit bone.

Her vision faded, winking out like an extinguished lamp, the pain almost throwing her into oblivion. She fought against the darkness. To pass out now would be death.

She reached out with her aching right hand and braced herself against a sharp edged tooth. The eel lifted her off the ground ready to toss down its meal.

Before it could swallow, Aminira thrust the blazing point of Ifrit through the roof of the beast's mouth, aiming, she prayed, at its brain. Aminira released the fireball into the eel-snake's flesh and yanked the blade free.

The eel-snake stopped and gagged. The black tunnel of its throat shuddered and pulsed. A burst of golden light broke the darkness of the monster's palette. A tiny gout of fire flickered out of the wound she'd made.

As Aminira watched, the flicker became a thick tongue that spread over the roof of the eel-snake's mouth. Suddenly everything was awash in flame and fire poured down the monster's throat. The blaze roared around Aminira and she clung to Ifrit. If she dropped the blade now she'd perish with the creature.

The eel-snake roared in pain blowing the flames around Aminira. She screamed as it shook its head. Its mouth opened and Aminira was thrown out. The tooth impaling her leg ripped free with a fresh burst of agony. She sailed through the air a moment, then hit stone.

Aminira rolled across the cave floor, every bruise and scrape and bounce a new torture. She came to rest on her back and she could see the eel-snake. The monster thrashed in the water, its entire head on fire. Aminira gaped, pain momentarily forgotten.

Ifrit's magical fire consumed the eel-snake's flesh. The eel's head was engulfed in an inferno. As she watched its lower jaw, burnt to charcoal, fell off and splashed into the water. The yellow eyes were gone, the eel's empty sockets poured orange fire and oily black smoke.

An agonized shriek echoed off the cave walls and for a second Aminira was sure the scream must have come from her. But no. She lay on the cold stone in silence, watching the eel-snake disintegrate. Aminira pushed herself up into a sitting position, the bloody rip in her leg stabbed with red-hot pain with every movement.

A few feet away, Aminira saw a grey heap. Yisabelle. The witch had collapsed. As the eel-snake's smoldering corpse at last sank into the water. She let out another, weaker cry. Was Yisabelle just mourning her monster? Or had the beast held a portion of her power. If so, this was Aminira's chance to strike.

The eel might be dead but if Yisabelle recovered before Aminira could get back on her feet she would be too. Aminira ripped the hem off her surcoat, tearing the raw silk. She tied the fabric around her bleeding leg. The blood flow was constant, alarmingly so, but the eel's fang had missed the artery. Aminira was still in danger of bleeding to death; the wound needed stitching. Right now she just needed to get up.

Using Ifrit's scabbard as a crutch, Aminira levered herself onto her feet. She hobbled over to the collapsed witch, dragging her injured leg. Yisabelle moaned and got to her knees just as Aminira arrived.

She grunted as Aminira pressed Ifrit's sharp edge against her neck. Then, to Aminira's surprise, Yisabelle laughed.

The witch sat back and looked up at Aminira. Blood streamed from her nose, eyes and ears. The whites of her eyes had gone red with broken blood vessels. Yisabelle sneered, lip curling over red stained teeth.

"You think you've won?" She snarled. "Look." She gestured with a shaking hand at the cavern.

Aminira pressed the blade harder against Yisabelle's throat and glanced away. The waterfalls still poured into the cave. The lake, the rivers, the water of Lagobel still drained away.

"There's only one way to break the curse and you'll never find it until it's too late. And when you do, you won't like the answer." Yisabelle coughed wetly and spit out blood.

"What do you mean?" Aminira asked. The old woman's pale skin turned grayer by the second. Perhaps she'd used some of her own life force to raise the eel-snake. Great magics often required great sacrifices.

"You'll never be together. You'll never be happy. No matter what you do, one of you will die," Yisabelle said.

"What do you mean?" Aminira demanded, voice growing harsh. The witch had to be wrong. How could any curse be so perfectly awful?

Yisabelle's only answer was a rattling sigh. Aminira shook her by the shoulder. "Tell me! Tell me what you mean." The witch's head lolled and she collapsed sideways. Aminira touched her throat, feeling for a pulse. Nothing. Yisabelle was dead and Aminira had no answers. Eadmund was as good as dead.

Aminira needed to be sure that Yisabelle could not cheat death. She pulled Ifrit back and swung. The blade cut effortlessly through the witch's neck. Blood oozed from the wound, spreading in a pool and mixing with the lake water. Yisabelle's final words echoed in Aminira's mind. They may prove true sooner than the witch anticipated. Defeat stung her eyes. The curse still held. The lake still emptied. And chances were, she would bleed to death before making it back to the castle kitchen. She could tear everything she wore to shreds for bandages and it still wouldn't staunch the flow.

There was nothing to close the wound with. She would have to pray God was kind and would see her up the cavern stairs. Ifrit would have to be her cane.

Ifrit. The sword could save her once again. Aminira sliced off the bandage and tore open her wide pants. She could not sew the wound shut but Ifrit could cauterize it.

For what she hoped was the last time today, Aminira called up Ifrit's power. The blade couldn't make another fireball but it didn't need to. The sword grew hot, hotter, and heat rippled the air around the blade.

When the blade was red hot, Aminira set the blade on the ground, keeping her hand on the hilt. When she released her grip Ifrit's fire could burn her. But the instant she let go the blade would begin to cool. She had to act fast. Aminira braced herself as best she could. Her breath came shallow and fast, making her ribs ache. She swallowed her fear and let go of the blade. Then she rolled her wounded leg over the red hot metal.

Agony, hotter than the sword, tore through her. She screamed but made sure Ifrit did its work. The stench of her own cooking flesh smothered her. When she could bear it no more she moved away from the blade and lay sobbing on the stone floor.

It felt like a long time before Aminira could think again. All thought had burned out of her mind as pain became her world.

Slowly, the ever present pain dulled enough to allow her thoughts to swim back.

She looked over the freshly cauterized wound in her leg and swallowed hard. The skin was blistered and raw like a poorly cooked hunk of meat. It would leave behind a long puckered scar if infection didn't kill her first.

Using the sheathed Ifrit to help herself up, Aminira limped toward the crack in the wall and beyond the stairs.

CHAPTER 11

Aminira woke, fell asleep, and woke again. For a moment she didn't remember if she had lived or died. She remembered crawling up the damp stone steps. She climbed for ages, hours, days, years. She wasn't sure. She blacked out several times, overwhelmed with pain and barely able to draw breath.

Above her soared an intricate stone ceiling. Was she in Heaven? Or perhaps still in Yisabelle's castle.

"Her Highness is awake," a voice cried out.

Was she awake, Aminira wondered? She blinked slowly and when she opened her eyes the worried face of Vizier Hamandir hovered over her, his dark eyebrows knit with concern. The creases on his brow deeper than usual.

"Princess Aminira, at last."

"At last?" she croaked and realized she was thirsty as the desert sands. "Water."

Another face appeared, a woman crinkled and brown as worn leather, a light blue scarf tied securely around her head.

"Physician?" the woman was from Aminira's own retinue, her royal surgeon, Hasna. This was Aminira's first need of the physician the entire trip. At least Aminira knew now she was indeed alive.

As if to give her further proof, Aminira was carefully propped up on more pillows, every movement awakening a pain somewhere in her body. At last she was upright and Dr. Hasna pressed a glass of water to her dry lips. She drank deeply and settled back into the cushions when she was done.

The unfamiliar room with its delicate stone work and diamond paned windows must be in Lagobel's palace. Aminira had no memory past climbing out of the cavern beneath Yisabelle's castle.

"How did I get here?" Aminira asked, voice a little stronger now she had water and was fully awake.

"My men brought you back," said a gruff voice from the open door.

King Luberto strode in. Though his face was worn with perpetual worry, he gave Aminira a tight smile.

She bowed as best she could in bed, inclining her head to the king while Vizier Hamandir and the doctor bowed low and stepped back.

"I told the men to leave if I didn't come back," Aminira said.

"They would never," Luberto said, pride puffing him up a bit. "And lucky for you they didn't listen. When they saw the castle's witch lights go out, they assumed Yisabelle dead. They waited longer but when you didn't come out, they went in after you. Found you unconscious in the kitchens."

"I am grateful for their bravery and persistence," she said.

"Is it true? Is Yisabelle dead? Eadmund has not recovered and the lake is nearly gone," said Luberto.

Aminira's hands twisted in the light summer blanket covering her. "Yisabelle is dead but I have failed," she admitted.

King Luberto hung his head a moment. "All is lost then. My son and Lagobel go to their deaths."

Her heart hurt in her chest, as if a dagger sliced it in two. Aminira would have liked to be alone then, so she could give in to the sobs that ached in the back of her throat. She had doomed the Prince she loved and his entire country with him.

She closed her eyes and saw Yisabelle's bloodied face spitting out her last vitriol. They would find an answer nearly too late. Where? What form would it take? Yisabelle told Aminira either she or the Prince would die. There was still the thinnest thread of hope left, more delicate than spider silk, and easier to snap. She dared not mention Yisabelle's words, especially in front of Vizier Hamandir. If he knew she could die, he would pack her up and take her away whether she wished it or not. Aminira had one ally yet who would not question orders.

"Is Bea about by any chance?" she asked. The girl was bound to have begged her way to the castle and Hamandir knew her fondness for the urchin.

The Vizier frowned. "Yes, she is. She's been sleeping outside in the hall these last two days."

"Two days? I've been unconscious that long?" Aminira said surprised. She thought only a day had passed.

"You needed the rest," Physician Hasna said.

"Indeed," Luberto agreed. "You were in a sorry state."

Aminira nodded. "I think I need more rest still. Would

you all mind leaving me with Bea for a moment? She can fetch anything I need."

They departed, King Luberto hunched, his bluster and energy gone. Once the room was empty, Bea was sent in. The girl smiled even as she wiped away a few tears.

"Princess." She took Aminira's hand and squeezed. Hasna had probably ordered her not to hug Aminira under any circumstances.

Aminira returned Bea's smile. "Tell me what happened while I slept."

Bea shook her head. "Nothing good. Crops dying and the herds will follow. His Majesty told the people to leave. And the prince, I heard, he never gets out of bed. Sleeps mostly and don't eat. All he drinks is boiled lake water and there's not much of that left. A few pools in the deeper parts."

Almost too late. Yisabelle's final words. Almost too late for the lake and for Eadmund.

"I'm so sorry you didn't save Prince Eadmund. It's not fair. You beat the witch and made it back." Tears shone in Bea's eyes.

Aminira touched Bea's head. The girl had taken to wearing a head scarf perhaps emulating Aminira, perhaps just to hide the stubble of her hair growing back.

"There may yet be hope," Aminira said.

"What?" Bea rubbed the unshed tears away.

"I didn't want to tell his majesty as nothing may come of it. But Princess Yisabelle said we could find the answer when it was almost too late." Aminira's empty stomach soured with guilt. She needed Bea, needed to use the girl's blind faith one last time.

A hopeful smile touched Bea's face and she asked, "What is it? What answer?"

"I don't know yet," Aminira said. She looked at the cotton blanket embroidered with pink roses so she wouldn't have to look Bea in the eye. "I think there might be something at the bottom of the lake that will break the curse. It all goes back to the lake." A lake now almost dry, its depths lying exposed.

"Like what?"

"I don't know. It could be anything. An amulet, a chalice, a rock. The witch didn't say. But it must be something that would stand out, that could be found when the lake is almost empty."

"I'll find it." Bea jumped up. "I can search the pools."

Of course, Aminira didn't have to ask. Bea was happy to help. Happy to do anything for her Princess. Aminira lay back and pulled the blanket around her, sick with guilt. Yisabelle's voice, harsh and cold, came to her again. One of you will die.

If Bea succeeded in her mission, found a way to break the curse, Aminira planned to use it. She would be the one to die. She would save Eadmund, save his Kingdom.

Could she do it? Would she really die for Eadmund? Perhaps the witch had read her heart truer than Aminira herself had. The idea of leaving beckoned her. She could go. She could even blame Hamandir. All she had to do was slip what Yisabelle said and he would command the royal guard to take her away for her own good. She wouldn't even be there when Eadmund died. Her stomach convulsed and the water almost came back up. Even if she couldn't or wouldn't save him and save his people, she had to be there when the end came. Duty and decency forbade her less. She may have condemned an entire kingdom to death. How could she live with herself if she did otherwise?

"One more thing, Bea. Tell no one what you are doing or why. If you find something in the lake, bring it straight to me." Bea nodded solemnly. Then her face twisted up as some unpleasant thought occurred to her.

"What is it?" Aminira asked.

"Well, the lake is huge, there's a lot of ground to cover..." she trailed off.

"Take a camel. They will be more sure-footed over rocks. And search the deepest pools first," Aminira said. Bea nodded but still looked concerned.

"Are you sure no one else can help?"

"I have faith in you, Bea," Aminira said. She settled back into the pillows and closed her eyes, unable to bare the girl's company any longer. Or perhaps it was her own guilt that made her head throb. "I need to rest. I'm sorry," she added. She heard the bedroom door open and shut as Bea quickly departed.

Four days went by as Bea searched.

Aminira told Vizier Hamandir that Bea would be with her in the palace running and fetching for her, and keeping her company. She told Hamandir to prepare the caravan to depart. He assumed they would leave when she was better and after Prince Eadmund had died.

She had ink and paper brought to her and she wrote out a will leaving instructions for Bea's welfare. A letter to her father and uncle were also written and sealed. She wanted to explain to her father what had happened to her and begged no harm should befall Vizier Hamandir who had been her good, loyal advisor during the journey.

Between sleeping and writing, she tested her leg. The long burn scar was pinkish and bright against her deep brown skin, too new to have darkened. The blisters were all but gone, leaving dead and peeling skin in their wake. If she was careful, Aminira could limp to the window and look out over the wilting gardens and dry lake bed.

Every morning Bea left to search among the rocks and pools from the docks, their beams now exposed. She rode out on a camel, her small frame bouncing with the camel's gait. Each evening Bea returned shaking her head as she told Aminira she'd found nothing.

Five more days passed while Bea searched the enormous lakebed. Aminira sat on a cushioned window bench, brow creased with concern and pain. Her ribs still ached and she thought her limp might be permanent, a constant reminder of her failure if Bea couldn't find whatever it was Yisabelle had been referring to. There could be too large an area to search for one person.

Aminira looked down at the dying garden. She had complimented it when she'd first arrived. Many of the flowers were turning brown, the ornamental ponds and fountains dry. She craned her neck, leaning over the open window sill. The prince's tower jutted over the lake, the balcony plunge he had described to her dropped away to a rocky death below.

She had the maids take him a message daily asking if she might see him one last time. Yisabelle's prophecy was coming true. One of them would die. Eadmund's death looked to be the most likely unless Bea succeeded soon.

Tears swelled and overflowed. Aminira let out a

shuddering breath, flaring pain reminding her of still broken ribs. Prince Eadmund refused to see her. The maids, grey faced and sober told her the prince barely moved, barely drank, wasting away as the lake dried. Aminira found it hard to imagine the young man she'd met only weeks ago, who demanded to be leapt off cliffs, lying in bed drained of life and energy.

The effort only hurt her more. She wished, almost desperately, to weep aloud but dignity and injury forced her to push aside her feelings.

Aminira wiped her tears away with a corner of her cotton sleeve. When she looked out at the lake again she saw a small figure approaching. Bea was back but it was only afternoon, normally she searched sunup to sundown. She sat up, leaning out the window. The camel's color and gait was unmistakable though Bea's dusty clothes made her look like an extension of the beast's hump.

Hope caught her breath. Sudden happiness swelled at the thought of her prince alive and well and whole. The momentary joy burst. If Bea had succeeded then her own death loomed before her.

What would it be? A vial of poison sunk to the bottom of the lake? An enchanted arrow to pierce her heart? Could she really go through with it? Aminira thought she would die of shame and sorrow if she did not try.

Aminira pushed aside her doubts. She must wait and see what Bea brought her. Perhaps the means of sacrifice would be swift and painless. Aminira rose from the window seat, anxious to pace. Her leg protested, pain racing up and down her thigh until effort and agony brought out a sheen of sweat on her forehead. She hobbled to the door and threw it open. The stone corridor had never looked so long.

She sat down heavily again and wiped her face.

At last Bea peered around the corner of the open door, even as she knocked politely on the door jam.

"Come, come," Aminira gestured her in.

Beaming and red-faced, Bea entered, flush from running through the great palace.

"I found something, just like you said." Bea opened the flap of a canvas satchel hanging heavily at her side. "I don't know what it is or what it says, but it's got to be what will break the curse."

The girl pulled out a golden tablet the size of a small dinner plate. It was thankfully thin or it might have weighed more than Bea could carry. The weight was significant when Aminira took the tablet from her.

"It's magic for sure," Bea said. "The writing keeps changing. I can't read none of it though. I plain can't read."

"We shall remedy that," Aminira said as she stroked a finger over the tablet's surface.

Bea was right about the text etched into the gold plate. As Aminira watched the words shifted from one language to another, then to a third. She waited breathlessly, hoping to recognize at least one.

On the fifth change, Aminira gasped. It was a language she knew. The tablet gave instructions to break Yisabelle's curse. The blood drained from Aminira's face and her heart beat hard and fast against paining ribs.

Only someone who loved the prince could save him. It was a trade. Her life for his. The directions made perfect, horrible sense. At the bottom of the pool where the tablet had been found was a hole through which the last of the lake drained. To save Prince Eadmund, someone who loved him must plug the hole with their hands and feet. The lake would then begin to fill. The curse would break when the person was drowned.

"Bea, go wait for me in the hall."

"What?"

"Go," Aminira shouted and instantly regretted it. Bea jumped up, and fled the room.

The thick oak door shut behind Bea and Aminira let out a sob. She dropped the tablet to the floor and put her head in her hands. All the emotions she'd been pushing aside for days, swelled and burst asunder. She wept, choking on tears, heedless of her bandaged ribs. What did it matter if they broke again? She welcomed the pain. All was misery.

Aminira let herself cry until her tears dried up. A few hiccupping sobs burst out once in a while but she was finally done.

Now she was decided on her course, Aminira dipped her fingertips in the pitcher of drinking water left for her, a day's ration only, and dabbed her face clean. She did not want Bea to know she'd been crying. She needed Bea's unquestioning cooperation.

Should she change clothes? A strange bit of vanity to occur to her. She looked down at her simple muslin garments. Should she change into fine silks and put on her best gems even though she would ruin them by drowning in them? Aminira decided they could dress her after.

Aminira put the will she had written and sealed with wax on the table beside the bed where it would be found. A cane had been left for her to help her walk any distance longer than her bedroom. She took it in hand and opened the door.

Bea sat in the corridor picking at the hem of her tunic. She scrambled to her feet as Aminira limped out.

"I am going to visit the prince and I will need your help. Then I want you to show me where you found the tablet."

"So the tablet had the answer?" Bea asked as they went slowly down the hall.

"It did indeed," Aminira said.

The walk from where Aminira had been quartered in the Palace and Prince Eadmund's suit should be a few minutes' walk. It took Aminira nearly twenty and her injured thigh hurt unrelenting. She remained silent on the subject, only pausing to rest at a couple of convenient chairs they came upon.

No one lingered in the wide stairwell outside the prince's rooms. The King and Queen, no doubt, kept from their dying son's bedside by the evacuation of an entire nation. Any guards they would have left on the door also likewise employed.

Princess Aminira limped to the prince's chamber door and tried the handle. It opened. She mopped the sweat from her face, her earlier washing had been useless. Pain and effort left her drenched, her limp worse than ever.

"Wait outside, Bea," she said.

"Sure you can make it?" Bea asked. The girl had had to help Aminira most of the way.

"There are no more stairs. I will be fine," Aminira said, then let herself into the prince's suite.

The curtains were drawn and only murky sunlight penetrated the thick fabric. Her eyes took a moment to adjust and Aminira stood just inside the door until she could see well enough to cross the room. If she fell down now she wasn't sure she could get back up again.

Leaning heavily on her cane, she went to the bedroom. It was just as dark and, for a moment, she thought the bed was empty. Then something moved listlessly under the covers.

"Prince Eadmund?" Aminira whispered. She rushed to the bed as fast as she was able and groped for a stool a maid had left. Aminira sat down hard.

The blanket moved again and his head poked from underneath. Aminira gasped when she saw him. He was wasted down to almost nothing. Cheek bones, high and sharp pressed through the flesh and grey skin sagged under his eyes.

He smiled and the chapped skin of his lips split. "What a pleasant dream, but you aren't to see me like this," Eadmund said, grey-blue eyes trying to focus on her.

Aminira felt her heart shatter. Fresh tears stung her eyes. He looked so nearly dead already. A corpse hanging onto life. She reached out and touched his hair, the sun-bleached golden thatch now brittle as straw. He didn't even lift his head from the pillow or try to sit up. She couldn't imagine he had the strength left to shift the rocks pinning the blanket over him.

"My fun princess," he whispered. "I wish we could go diving again."

"You will." She managed to choke out the words, her throat aching to weep again. "I'm going to break the curse. You will live and be happy."

"I'm dying." He shook his head weakly and his eyes closed. "You can jump up into the lake for me."

"You won't die," Aminira said, voice firm and louder than she intended. "But I must say goodbye."

His eyes opened again. "Goodbye? But you must come back."

"No. I will never see you again, nor you me." Impulsively, Aminira leaned in and kissed his dry forehead. It felt like bone beneath her lips. But it was one less thing not to regret–that she had never kissed him.

"You will feel better soon my prince," Aminira said as she heaved herself to her feet. "Just wait a few hours and you'll see. Goodbye."

Aminira hobbled out, leg in all the more pain from having rested a moment. She did not turn or pause even as Eadmund called for her to wait. She could not. Every minute that passed what little was left of the lake, drained away, taking his life with it.

She reached the corridor and Bea gasped when she saw Aminira.

"You're crying," the girl blurted.

"Am I?" Aminira wiped her face with her hand. "It's nothing. I'm only sorry to see the prince look so ill. Now. I need you to take me to where you found the gold tablet."

"Right now?"

"Yes," Aminira said and limped for the stairs without waiting for Bea's reply.

The camel sat to let Princess Aminira and Bea mount and for once Aminira was grateful for the cantankerous beasts. She could never have mounted a horse with her injured leg. As it was, the camel's wild teeter front then back, as it stood up, drove hot pokers of agony into all Aminira's injuries.

Her vision swam and blackened, and she clung to Bea

to keep from falling. The camel leveled out once on his feet and Aminira recovered herself.

The trip across the rocky lake bed was not a comfortable one. Much of the bottom was thick, cracked mud dried by the sun. Dead fish, unscavenged, lay about in rocky formations that only a few days ago held pools of water. Water weeds rotted in fly covered heaps. Birds of prey circled overhead. Once in a while an eagle or hawk would drop from the cloudless sky and fly off with a dead fish.

They passed islands that rose like hillocks over their heads. The pines that had once thrived there, now rusty red, their needles fallen to the dry grasses. A few shallow pools still remained; foul with the dead fish who had gathered there.

Aminira pulled her head scarf up over her nose though it didn't help keep out the thick gagging smell of death. Near palpable clouds of stench hovered over the lake bed, thick as the flies, the last thriving life the lake had to offer.

"I am very sorry to have sent you to search the lake," she said to Bea through clenched teeth, trying not to heave over the side of the camel. "I have used your generosity and kindness ill. I did not know or think the lake bed would be like this."

Bea shook her head. "I'm happy to help you. I just hope we aren't too late. With the curse broken you can marry Prince Eadmund."

Princess Aminira said nothing more, too guilty to trust herself not to tell Bea the entire terrible plan. The girl would no doubt try to stop her from sacrificing herself. She was too young to understand Aminira's duty, but old enough to know betrayal.

Aminira tried to swallow the swelling lump in her throat.

She had run from turmoil once before. Left her loved ones behind to face whatever fate and God had in store. She could not do it again. And she wasn't sure she could stand firm in the face of Bea's pleading. And she knew, with stinging sadness, that she had indeed used the girl for her own ends since they had met on the street. First she had needed directions, but then she had needed a friend and then an unwitting conspirator. All of which Bea gladly became for her princess. A princess unworthy of such devotion.

The camel rounded an island, the base and shore of which were littered with huge boulders sloping to a steep depression. Bea brought the beast up short and patted its sandy colored neck.

At the bottom of the depression was a wide, shallow pool, its few small fish still alive. More boulders poked out of the water, dried to the color of bones.

"That's the pool the tablet was in." Bea pointed down the slope.

"Then here is where you leave me," Aminira said.

"What? No. Can't I stay and watch?" Bea looked over her shoulder at Aminira.

"No," Aminira said. "I must do this alone."

Unconvinced, Bea fretted a moment, worried eyes fixed on Aminira's face.

"I will get down myself," Aminira said and gripped the wooden saddle frame. She could perhaps slide down over the camel's rump, though it was a long drop.

"No," Bea said. She gave the camel the command to sit and the beast, grumbling, went to its knees.

"Are you sure I can't stay?" Bea asked. "How will you get back?"

"You can tell the King's men where I am in the morning."

"What about Vizier Hamandir? He'll ask me where you are. Shall I tell him?"

"No, tell no one," Aminira snapped. "My orders are this: Go back to the palace and hide the gold tablet. Tell no one where I am until dawn. I am sorry and grateful to you for everything, dear Bea. But you must do this last thing for me."

The girl looked momentarily surprised. Then her eyes hardened. At last she nodded. "All right."

"Thank you Bea. For all you have done. And I want you to know you have a future with my people if you choose it." With a groan Aminira dismounted. There was thankfully a smooth topped boulder near her feet and she let herself down more easily than she had gotten up.

Aminira waited until the camel rose again and Bea started back to the castle before slowly climbing down the crusty rocks to the pool below.

The rocky descent to the pool of water was slow and excruciating. Her injuries forced her to rest several times on the way down. More than once she had to resort to the undignified move of sitting and scooting down a boulder on her rear, unable to climb. Aminira pushed the pain away. Only a few more minutes and she would reach the pool, then everything would end.

At last her sandaled feet dipped into the warm slimy water of the shallows. Panting, but unwilling to put off the deed, Aminira plunged her hands into the muddy fetid water, hands searching for the hole the tablet described. The pool of water was small and she quickly found it at the base of a smooth flat-topped boulder.

Princess Aminira sat down with a long pained sigh. The hole at the bottom of the lake formed a rough triangle. The widest point was closest to the stone and big enough that her feet could fit inside. She put her feet in and felt a gentle suction pulling water between her toes. The pool was likely hours from draining away entirely.

Her feet alone couldn't cover the hole and she had to stop the water flowing completely. Aminira leaned down to cover the remaining corner with her hand. The suction increased, but water still slid around her feet. Aminira reached into the water and unbuckled her sandals. She tossed them aside and repositioned her feet. That did it. Her feet and hands were sucked tight against the stone. The water no longer slipped over her skin. The hole was completely blocked off, and according to the tablet, the lake should begin to fill again. The curse would be broken.

Aminira wondered how long it would be before she saw a result. She hoped for the lake to fill quickly, but she watched the water and saw no change in the water level. What a slow, horrible death she had volunteered for. Doubts wormed their way into her thoughts as the flies buzzed around her. Would she really sit there and sacrifice herself? Simply wait to drown? Each time she felt tempted to pull her hands or feet away, the image of Prince Eadmund dying in his bed, rose in her mind. His wasted body and waxen skin, the tan faded away by illness and a lack of sun.

The best Aminira could do was shut her eyes and try not to think at all. She listened to the distant cry of hawks and eagles. Focused on the tickle of flies walking across her forehead, occasionally shaking them off, only to have them return seconds later.

Gradually she became aware of another soft, rhythmic sound, so faint and regular she wasn't sure when it had begun.

Aminira opened her eyes. Tiny wavelets lapped at her

feet and she swore the water had risen. Not much, but it had crept up to the arch of her feet. As she watched the water rose a bit more, like a slow tide creeping higher over the beach.

She stared into the water, the color of black coffee, and tried to discern the rate the water rose. Aminira sat so still the listless small fry trapped in the pool with her swam over to investigate. They took experimental nibbles at her toes to see if they were edible.

Afternoon sun warmed her back and the rocks threw heat at her from all directions. Aminira felt at home for the first time since leaving and with her eyes closed she could imagine herself at a desert oasis, her feet cooling in the water with date palms swaying overhead.

The water tickled her ankles and Aminira opened her eyes again. The cuffs of her loose pants were wet. The lake seemed to be filling a bit faster.

A line of slick wetness could be seen on the rocks where the water splashed a little higher. The water closed over her ankles. Aminira gauged the time by the shadow of the boulders. She guessed that the lake would reach over her head a little past sunset. Though it would be too late for her by then. The water need only reach past her nose.

Again she shut her eyes and shoved all feelings away. She focused on the dancing lights and shifting colors behind her eyelids. Poems and songs floated into her mind, all of them melancholy. She recited them to herself, including several prayers for the dead. She hoped King Luberto's men would find her corpse before it was too bloated and ugly. Then chided herself for her vanity.

The sun passed slowly overhead, every hour the water rose. Aminira drowsed in the heat. Her dreams dwelt on her father and uncle who she desperately wished to see one last time, and her mother, may God keep her, who Aminira would be joining soon in death.

She woke sobbing several times. Her tears dripped down her nose and fell, making tiny ripples as they joined the water below.

Between such fitful naps, she watched as the lake came back to life. The small fish fry hovered around her seat waiting for flies, drawn by Aminira's sweat, to come low over the water so they could snatch them from the air.

Birds landed and drank. Handsome hawks and eagles that reminded her of the first time she came upon the lake with Rana. Crows landed next, their raucous cries bringing more silky black birds. Small panting song birds followed the crows.

By the time the water reached waist high on Aminira, the pool, sunk in its rocky depression, was in full shadow. She could see golden rays touching the tops of the brittle trees high above her, but the lake bed was deep and she was at the bottom.

Later still, after another sleep from which a cramp in her shoulder woke her, Aminira saw deer drinking at the edge of the pond. The sky above faded from sunset bright to indigo with a few stars just beginning to twinkle.

Aminira shivered as the water closed over her shoulders, wetly creeping toward her neck. Not long now. She closed her eyes and prayed the evening cants. The last she would ever make. Thanking God and His mercy for the day, then added a final prayer for a swift death. Her cotton head scarf floated around her, lifted by the water, which now tickled her chin.

Minutes left. She squeezed her eyes shut and thought of Prince Eadmund. His laughter, his smile, the warmth of his skin in her arms. Eadmund, beautiful as a marble statue in the moonlight. His delight as they danced at the ball.

Aminira tried to fight the panic with her memories but everything was wiped away when the water lapped against her mouth. She strained her aching neck, trying to keep her face clear of the water.

High above, Aminira heard the crunch of gravel and clatter of rocks. More deer come to drink, or something larger? The deer had not made such noise. A bear perhaps. Maybe an animal would kill her before she drowned. What of the curse then?

"Princess Aminira?" Eadmund's voice called over the rim of the depression.

Every nerve in Aminira's body tingled as hope scoured her like a sandstorm. She was saved. She must die. She was not alone. She didn't want to die in front of him.

"You lied to me." Bea's high pitched voice, cracked with sobs.

A weak laugh echoed the remark.

Then they were there. Aminira felt her hope crack in half, and a desperate ache welled up in its place. They weren't supposed to be here. She was to die alone, to spare them the anguish of watching her drown, but somehow they were here.

Silhouetted against the last orange of the sky, a camel trotted up to the rim, Bea on his back and Prince Eadmund flying out behind, hanging from a rope tied to the back of the saddle.

"Are you still alive?" Bea called down, a note of accusation in her voice.

Aminira bit into her cheek to keep from answering. She shook her head and water splashed around her.

"I hear water," the prince said.

The camel sat down with a bellow and Bea leaped off. "She's there at the bottom!"

Prince Eadmund pulled himself along the rope and grabbed up a couple of stones from the ground.

"Go away," Aminira screamed at them, desperate for them to leave. Already her courage was draining away and her muscles strained to pull her feet from the hole she plugged. She refused to let go now. Not with the proof of Eadmund's safety standing right before her.

"You can't die and leave me." Bea sobbed against the side of the camel.

"The girl is right," Prince Eadmund said. "I'm feeling much better now, come up." He chuckled.

"It's not done. Take Bea and leave," Aminira shouted. She spit out some water that got into her mouth. She would not be able to speak much longer.

Throwing himself off the lip of the hollow, he descended slowly, weighted by the stones in his hands. He landed in ankle deep water, and tossed aside the stones as he waded out to her.

He knelt in front of her, the water almost waist high on him. "Come away," he said again, softer, a ghost of his old, jovial smile playing on his lips. "When the lake is full we can go diving again."

"You don't understand," she said. "The tablet."

"The tablet is foolishness. I read it in your room. I felt so much better, I wanted to tell you and found it there, and I'm sure it is lying if it came from Yisabelle." Eadmund giggled and shook his head. "So you can leave off this silliness."

His smile remained fixed but strained. Aminira wasn't sure but she thought she saw the stirrings of other emotions in his eyes. The only consolation Aminira could take from their arrival was that the curse was breaking. Her actions weren't in vain, it was working. He would live and be whole and have his gravity back.

"You feel better because the curse is lifting. All the more reason I cannot move." Aminira had to speak out of the side of her mouth, the water had risen nearly to her nose.

"But you cannot mean to—" He struggled with something deep inside himself. Eadmund's smile twitched, faltering for the first time. "If you don't move now you will...you will..." He couldn't bring himself to say the words 'drown' or 'die'. They clashed so with the buoyancy that had been his permanent state for so long.

Instead, Eadmund grabbed Aminira's shoulders and tugged, trying to pull her free. Aminira tried to shake him off, the frothing water splashed over her nose as they fought silently.

In the struggle, Aminira realized she was stuck fast to the bottom of the lake. The suction she had first felt when she put her feet and hands into the hole, had strengthened. Not painfully so, but no ordinary strength would pry her loose as the prince was trying to do. This was part of a spell and the magic would have the life it was owed.

The water crested Aminira's nose and she tried to keep her head up. Despite all intentions, she instinctively fought to live.

Seeing that, Prince Eadmund dove into the water. She felt him clawing at her feet and hand trying to pull them free.

Bea sobbed uncontrollably and scrambled down the side of the depression. "Don't give up! We'll save you!"

Eadmund's hands scraped at her hands and feet but nothing budged her. He surfaced and grabbed Aminira's face and tried to tug it high enough for her to breathe.

But the water rose and the task was impossible. Aminira's lungs hurt, the air in them fast burning away.

Unwilling to let her go, he held her head up, trying to keep her out of the water. He stared into her eyes, his own wide enough the whites shown all around.

"Do not leave me," he whispered. His smile broke apart then reasserted itself.

Aminira trembled with effort not to breathe, but there was no help for it. She had no last thought or feeling other than dreadful panic.

The reborn lake crawled up to her eyes and she squeezed them shut. And at last, there was nothing but her body's instinct to inhale.

Water rushed into her mouth and nose, choking her. Aminira convulsed, her free hand clung to Eadmund.

Pain seared her lungs. The last of her panic bled away. Into darkness.

Sometimes she was hot. Then cold. She skimmed the surface of consciousness never quite breaking through. Voices came to her. Soft sobs and mutterings. Sometimes Aminira thought her eyes were open and she could see grey light. Most of the time she was absent or the world was. Long black stretches deeper than sleep, during which she felt time must have passed but there was no knowing how much or if it was a hallucination.

She drifted back to wakefulness, pulled by a gentle sound she had not enough intelligence yet to name.

Her eyes cracked open, pierced by gently diffused light.

She had drowned. Aminira remembered the terrified choking, the lack of air. The consuming fear. She squeezed her eyes shut and felt warm tears trickle down the sides of her face.

Aminira breathed in to reassure herself that she took in only air, and felt a rattle in her chest. The rattle became an itch, so unbearable and forceful, a coughing fit seized her.

Hands helped her upright and pushed a handkerchief under her lips. They stroked her back as great wracking phlegmy coughs shook her until her body hurt beyond words.

At last the cough resulted in a glob of greenish phlegm, forcibly expelled. The handkerchief was folded up and born swiftly away.

Aminira fell back on a nest of pillows and turned to the person who had helped her.

She gasped and nearly brought on another coughing fit. Prince Eadmund sat by her beside. He had not died, and yet she lived. Shock numbed her fever riddled brain. She gaped at him, gasping for breath that wetly rattled in her aching chest.

The prince pulled a handkerchief from a pile on the bedside table and wiped at his eyes. He sniffled and smiled at her sadly.

"Welcome back," he said and took her hand.

As Aminira watched, tears rained from his eyes. She reached out and touched his face, amazed to see him cry.

Eadmund let her hand rest on his face a moment then he took her hand in his.

"The curse is broken, thanks to you," he said.

"How?" she croaked.

"You drowned," he said. "And when you did, everything, everything inside me just… changed. I felt—" he shook his head. "I felt everything I'd never felt before, and pulled you from the water, put you over a boulder, and pressed the water from your lungs." A sob broke off his story and he wiped the handkerchief across his face without letting go of her hand.

He cried a few minutes, sniffled, blew his nose, and smiled at her. "Wu-Pei says I am crying all the tears I never shed while cursed." He laughed, a soft rueful sound, humor mixed with resignation. "Hopefully I will not be at this another twenty years."

Aminira's chest constricted as she fought back her own tears of joy. If she began to cry now, she would likely only cough herself to death.

"Bea and I brought you back to the castle. You've been ill for days. An infection in the lungs."

Eadmund turned to her, clutched her hand in both of his and said, "I know you cannot promise never to die, but please, promise never to leave me again."

It was a moment before Aminira could speak. She had never felt so swamped by joy, so overcome. Words and thought seemed beyond her and she wished she could show Eadmund her heart, which seemed to glow inside her. He stared at her as her silence stretched on, concern, then doubt, knitting his brow.

She coughed, not so hard this time, only to clear her throat, and asked, "Will you marry me then?"

His face brightened, transfigured with joy. "Of course I'll marry you! That's exactly the thing!" he exclaimed, then paused. "Only..."

"Only what?"

"We shall have to wait until you are well and I have learned to walk. Turns out having gravity and going about on the ground all the time are not so easy. My legs are very weak."

"Neither will take long," Aminira said.

"I hope not," he fretted.

He looked so concerned she couldn't help a chuckle and reached up, pulling his face close to hers. "I came back from death, a month's delay is nothing," she said, then tilted her head, ready to steal a kiss from her fiancé.

The door banged open and Bea marched into the room. Aminira blushed and released Eadmund quickly before her impropriety ran away with her.

"I'm happy you didn't die," Bea announced as she halted by the bed, hands balled into fists. "I was so angry when His Highness read the tablet and it said you had to die. You should have told me."

"I'm deeply sorry, Bea. I know I used you and you deserve so much better. I will forever have the burden of it."

Bea nodded. "Prince Eadmund said I should forgive you since you saved his life."

"And will you forgive me, Bea?" Aminira asked sincerely. She remembered the girl sobbing into the side of the camel as she drowned.

"I will," Bea answered with all seriousness. "But only

because I was right. And because you didn't die. If you had, I never could."

"Thank you, Bea. I am grateful. And just wait, you shall have a herd of camels all your own."

A heavy sigh of disapproval from the doorway announced Vizier Hamandir's arrival. He stood glaring at them all, arms crossed. "I suppose this means we will be staying," he said.

THE END

ABOUT THE AUTHOR

Che Gilson is the author of Avigon and Avigon: Gods and Demons, graphic novels published by Image Comics and illustrated by Jimmy Robinson. She went on to write Dark Moon Diary volume 1 and 2 published by TOKYOPOP and illustrated by Brett Uher. Her short fiction has appeared twice in Luna Station Quarterly. Most recently her urban fantasy novella Carmine Rojas: Dog Fight and novel Tea Times Three, a contemporary fantasy, both published by Black Opal Books. Her passion is fantasy, witches, monsters werewolves and witches. Besides writing, she loves to take photos of moss and is lucky to live in the Pacific Northwest where moss grows on literally everything.